The Zygote Chronicles

SUZANNE FINNAMORE

The Zygote Chronicles

Grove Press
New York

Published simultaneously in Canada
Printed in the United States of America

FIRST EDITION

Library of Congress Cataloging-in-publication Data

Finnamore, Suzanne.
     The zygote chronicles / by Suzanne Finnamore.
        p. cm.
     ISBN 0-8021-1706-6
     1. Pregnant women—Fiction.   I. Title.

PS3556.I4965 Z94 2002
813'.54—dc21   2001040706

Grove Press
841 Broadway
New York, NY 10003

02 03 04 02   10 9 8 7 6 5 4 3 2 1

For P.

Zygote: fertilized egg; incipient organism, embryo, fetus

Not without the grace of heaven were you born and bred.

—Homer, *The Odyssey*

~

It was in July that we began trying to conceive. Initially it was very exciting. We told people, they would congratulate us as though you were on your way over in a cab. There was need for lavish carnal activity, sanctioned by God.

Six months went by. Where were you, we wondered, newly humbled. Already you had clout, kept people waiting. There were no guarantees you would show at all: a diva.

"We're trying," we said.

Almost Christmas then, that zing in the air. I met your father in the Presidio for hamburgers and red wine. I recall light confidences, an overall air of gladness, the evening's hard slant of sun as we walked in. Later we slipped home to our yellow bedroom and you happened. Joe DiMaggio was at the bar at Lil's that night. I surely don't consider this a coincidence.

On the eighth day of the new year, the line on the home-pregnancy stick became a pink cross, an almost papal confirmation. Looking at it, I felt a crazy glee. Terror, but no real surprise. For days I'd had a physical sense of you, like someone standing behind me at a party.

That night your father came home and instantly ferreted out the test stick from the top of my rolltop desk. He ran upstairs, clutching it like a white plastic flag high above his head, triumphant. I remember that he ran. I remember it was a Thursday. The next day he started worrying about money and being forty-nine and wringing his hands, but that night was pure. Slowly we danced to Andrea Marcovicci, the evidence of you fresh. We went to bed early, clothes and shoes peppered across the floor. We rushed as though to join you.

There has been a great deal of stick-urinating on your behalf. The ovulation sticks, which didn't work, and the pregnancy sticks, which did. Now let there be an end to all stick-urinating.

The song we danced to was "It Might Be You."

~

Thirty-four weeks yet to go, I am thinking as we wind down the mountain and the moss-draped madrone trees lean out to greet us. It is called Madrone Canyon because of the trees' abundance, beautiful and lithe, growing at times parallel to the ground. They were here before us and will be here when we are gone. We are canyon dwellers, we three.

At the bottom of this mountain is a public park, nestled within a very bossy clutch of California redwoods that the road dissects. Its name is Dolliver, but because of the immense shady trees, the locals call it Dark Park. This is not meant to be a negative; darkness can be soothing. It's dark where you are now.

Dark Park has monkey bars, slides, and the thing that goes around and around that all the mothers are afraid of. There's a low pebbly creek, and several picnic benches within the seasoned redwood grove. It's all been arranged. The trees and the park and the creek are waiting for you, they have so much patience I feel somewhat shamed. Of course, it's easy to be patient when you're a tree.

Low in my body I feel something I must imagine: a tingling, gritty sensation. On the car stereo, your father plays a song for you. "Please Call Me, Baby," by Tom Waits.

Please call me, baby, wherever you are
It's too cold to be out walkin' in the streets . . .

Your father says that you are not a classical baby, you are a blues baby.

This is what he looks like, your father: dark brown hair mingled with gray, soft skin that tans easily, silver glasses. Of average height, a primarily kind face with heavily lidded eyes that affect boredom but hoard interest. Women have always liked him. I liked him myself, liked him so much I married him. Watch out for this kind of thing.

I will tell you something else about your father. I was worrying about becoming ugly in his eyes. And he said, "Don't worry about getting big, because every month you are going to get more beautiful. And every month I will love you a little more."

I waited for him before I had you. Or maybe it was you who waited.

My best friend, Diana, is pregnant, her due date exactly a month ahead of mine. Be advised that you are in fact part of a diabolical scheme to have our babies at the same time and then go on to rule the world. At the very least we'll be large and threatening together. People will stand aside on the street when they see us coming, as a matter of practicality if not outright respect.

Diana and I met during the first day of junior high school in Oakland, California, in Mr. Cramer's American history class. Mr. Cramer looked like a hipster Santa Claus with brown hair and horn-rimmed glasses. He eventually ran away with a student, which I guess is as good a lesson in American history as any. Diana ran away to Los Angeles, New York, and finally to New Mexico, where she fell in love with her husband, but not before we became best friends and shared a few life-threatening escapades, all of which we now treasure like precious stones.

Diana will be your favorite older person. I know this in advance. Diana has red-gold hair, a deep voice, large Slavic features, and perfect skin. She will be the woman standing next to your mother holding drinks, this is how you will know her. Now is

Diana's second pregnancy. Her daughter, Carmen, was born the year your father and I became engaged. Carmen is twice as tall and gorgeous as a three-year-old girl frankly has a right to be. She is whip smart and, if bribed even slightly, will get coffee for us.

Last spring Diana and I were on the phone exploring the idea of conception, and I said, "Well, we've got to have a deadline." Diana said, "When?" and I said, "January one. Ninety-eight." I was firm about it, as I recall. I held one arm up high in the air.

Diana was already a veteran. This led to many long conversations regarding ovulation and which precise points we were at in our cycles, and did anyone really know anything. We exchanged stories about who had gotten pregnant and on what day in their cycle they had done it. We talked about what days we did it last month and what days we were going to try this month. We did everything but break out the chicken blood and hoodoo sticks.

Your father did not join in these debates and was never concerned in the slightest that I would conceive. He had a faith that bordered on Catholicism, a firm belief that I could conceive at any time of any month. I think he genuinely thought it would take only one month, but it didn't. He was philosophical, I was cautiously optimistic. By that time we were having a lot of sex, which in and of itself was engaging. There are worse things than taking off all your clothes in the middle of the day and making a baby. It's not high on the list of unpleasant things to do.

After a few months Diana and I decided to become scientific; this meant daily personal phone calls from our offices and the use of ovulation sticks, which had worked for two teachers at her school but not for her sister. We would actually put the phone down, take the ovulation test, wash our hands, and come back to the phone to report our findings. Between ovulation analysis, sexual target dates, and general folklore, it was not unusual for us to spend an hour at a stretch on the line. We had the zeal and camaraderie of professional athletes. And we made it. She conceived around November 20, and I conceived around December 22. It doesn't get much tighter than that. Considering this now, I feel incredibly able. I know it was entirely up to you, the moment you decided to materialize here in the global asylum, but allow me this feeling of power. It may be the last time.

Months earlier I'd found a smooth white stone and written the word *hope* on it in red pencil. I placed it in our front yard, on a large rock next to the rosemary bush. When the first rains knocked the stone down into the dirt, by the roots of the sage bush, I brought it back up onto the rock. I gave it a place in the sun. Every so often now, I check to see if I can still read the word on it. It is still there.

I'm going to tell you about us, so you won't feel uninformed later. Ignorance is the backbone of oppression.

I work in advertising, as does your father. In the writing profession, advertising is the least work you can do for the most money. It has the benefit of being occasionally fun, all the while possessing the moral center of a Turkish prison. Advertising means drinking espresso and buying many CDs you don't have to pay for, and then at the last possible second having an idea that involves either the Eiffel Tower or pyramids. It means attending foreign independent films and discerning which unique or especially touching parts you can fashion into a hot-dog commercial. It is long, surreal meetings in which people wearing terribly expensive watches passionately debate the personality of bleach.

Advertising is pitching a large television campaign to a middle-aged white man wearing a puka-shell necklace while your partner sits crooked on his chair, wordlessly eating a bag of Cheetos, viciously hung over with one side of his hair sticking straight up.

If at any time during your presentation the puka-shell man laughs, then you know you're going to full production. You're moving into full production even though you don't have scripts, because this is the kind of client who gets furious if there are scripts, because then he can't write his own campaign during the presentation. Which is what he's doing now as he says, "Yes. And the older man is helping the *younger* man paint the wall, instead of walking by." "Yes," you say. "*Celebrate* the product," he murmurs. "Yessssss..." you say, coaxing a skittish dog into a car. "I love it," the Token Lesbian in the Position of High Power says; and everyone at the table is beaming now, your best friends in the world instead of what they were at the presentation last week, which was hillbillies with guns.

Once you are in production, advertising means a forty-year-old commercial director in a porkpie hat who has people bring him chai and talks about *the process* in hushed church tones. All the while saying no to everything the client asks for, especially if it means showing the product in any way. His wife will visit the set; she will be ten.

Much of this used to matter to me, what campaign got produced, who directed it, the proximity of whatever hotel everyone was currently staying at. Keeping away from the shunned hotels. But now it is fading with remarkable speed. I seem to be admiring it all from a distance. For the first time in my career, I am not wondering what the next step is. I know what the next step is. *Out*. I am getting on the baby ship. I am the baby ship.

~

I fell in love with your father with terrible swiftness. Within five minutes I thought, I could marry this man. Not in the sense that he was easy, but in the sense that I could love him that long and hard. I imagined there would be laughter involved. With laughter I felt I could endure marriage. How simple it seemed, how imperative. I was compelled to make a fast decision, as though God were playing blackjack with me for my own happiness, my life. I had to say, Hit me, God. Hit me.

It wasn't his demeanor that drew me to him. It was evening, he was tired and, I think, despondent. It wasn't charm or physical sheen, it was what I saw inside of him, signaling to me behind his eyes in a way he may not have been aware of. And I've felt basically lucky ever since, almost every day of my life. That's something else love should make you feel. It should make you feel fortunate.

It will be made clear to you in a stray gesture, the line of a throat. Something in the hands. There may or may not be any music playing. But there will be a certain velocity of the spirit, a sensation of dropping through clear space unimpeded, and you think, This is the one. I found you.

Today I called a friend to talk about you, and then I realized she was grotesquely unworthy. I never trusted her, she has this very competitive habit of vibe-ing me: if I have a hangnail, she's got gangrene. If I have cramps, she's having not just the heaviest period of her life but what she suspects is an early miscarriage. If I say there is a Mafia hit man in my living room holding a knife to my eye, she'll say, "So? I've had Mafia hit men holding knives to my eyes all my life." I've known this, but it took being pregnant to realize it fully.

I can see you're already this very small and tight Committee, and the Committee will say where we are going and where we aren't. What's good to eat and what isn't. Finding food that is good to eat has become a troublesome adventure. Almost nothing is as good as it should be, or as good as I remember it. Whereas before I was happy to eat whatever was put in front of me, I can't now. It has to pass each newly heightened sense, or most of them. There seem to be electoral votes involved. Twice this week I have ordered take-out pizza, eaten one bite, and thrown the whole thing away. Olives have taken on an insidious presence, as have green bell peppers. Instead of being mild facilitators, now they destroy everything they touch.

The Committee decided I wasn't going to be smoking anymore. And I thought it was me making that decision, because I didn't even know I was pregnant at that time, though I wanted to be. I stubbed out my last Marlboro Light on New Year's Eve; a brave and personal resolution, or so I thought. Now I know that you had just burrowed yourself into my uterus lining and had decided that nicotine was unacceptable. *Fin.*

I am just past eight weeks pregnant. I take hold of my cast-iron skillet, its heft alone enormously satisfying. I melt a nub of butter in the blackness, crack an egg on its hard, capable side; like most women, I admire a cooking implement that has the ability to maim. It was William Burroughs who said that no one owns life, but anyone with a frying pan owns death.

I scramble two jumbos, look at them, and suddenly they don't look like eggs. They appear to be precisely what they are, which is pulverized dead baby chicks: aborted chickens that had no chance to live, to see the world. Gazing into the viscous embryonic pool, I can almost hear their feathery screams. I may also possibly see an eye. Fueled by a rush of zealot hormones, an unnaturally harsh reality is emerging.

After cramming the pulverized chicks down the garbage disposal, I lie down in the bedroom as intensely purposeful enzymes race through my body like tiny malicious joyriders. One minute later, your father is lurking in the doorway, bouncing on the balls of his feet, saying he wants to see a matinee. Insisting that I rise and dress, that we leave right away. The smell of the popcorn alone would send me over the edge. As I contemplate this, I advance-sense the fake rancid-butter odor slipping up my nostrils until I almost retch.

It's eleven A.M. and I can't get out of my cat-hairy bathrobe. I feel like I drank nine martinis last night aboard a badly driven submarine, and your father wants me to snap out of it and see a film. He says *The New York Times* liked it, and to bring a plastic bag in case I need to vomit.

The first thing you need to know about humankind is that we are somewhat selfish. Rapacious would not be an overstatement. Once you grasp this simple truth, you hold the key to mankind. If there's a single space in the lifeboat and you are standing next to anyone but to anyone but Ghandi or your natural parents, expect a struggle. Men in particular are capable of remarkable acts of selfishness performed on a consistent basis over long periods of time. Examples include Napoleon, Adolf Hitler, Donald Trump, and the methodical extinction of almost everything on Earth. Even the best of men, like your father, are centered on themselves in a way most women can only contemplate.

Here it is Saturday morning, and I have found a modicum of relief from the harsh nausea and the egg madness by reclining in bed with my laptop and e-mailing Mad Augusten in New York. Your father is there in the doorway, seeming vaguely unlike the fine man I know and perpetually welcome the sight of: now he looks as though he should have a long, low black hat and a poker of some kind. He is saying I never want to go anywhere anymore. He is calling me dull, so I call him inconsiderate. We don't actually say these things, we imply. Along with extended stretches of contentment and occasional bursts of joy, this is some of what you can anticipate when you grow up and get married. Baby, *no one* expects it to happen to them.

If you are a girl, I don't think you should necessarily become a lesbian, although if the idea appeals to you, I wouldn't say anything *against* it. I wouldn't try to stop you. Men can be obstinate and difficult to live with. Unlike myself, a perfectly reasonable woman unless shown a bag in which I am to place my vomit.

If you are a boy, I apologize.

Mad Augusten is a thirty-two-year-old writer with a warm smile and the eyes of a serial killer. He lives in Manhattan and has never cooked a meal in his entire life, not even tinned soup. Instead he orders beef vindaloo, Cantonese lobster with ginger sauce, pork rangoon, and something called salad pizza. He pays for it, eats it, and leaves the cartons in his living room, every inch of which is piled with books. He has an eighth-grade education and has sold several books to major publishers; the first he wrote in two weeks. He once performed oral surgery on himself at three A.M. with a thumbtack and a large Scotch. He dates a man whom he has been seeing for years but is not his boyfriend, because Mad Augusten is too crazy to have a boyfriend. He falls in love with people and destroys them without actually meaning to, an absentminded knife thrower, a blind pilot.

He has a single Calphalon stock pot in the middle of his living room because his light fixture leaks when it rains.

"Are you on the top floor?" I asked him.

"No," he said. "That's what disturbs me."

You should have at least one friend like this, possibly more. Life absolutely requires the occasional unhinged artist.

Professionally, I am investigating my options. My assistant, K., is helping me. We are examining the official documents of corporate policy as it relates to years employed and time spent away from the job at full pay. We are cackling and fondling the shiny saddle-stitched corporate rule book and calculating the exact parameters of maternity leave. The timing of my employment and your conception have dovetailed in a bizarre yet fortuitous way: by accident, your mother has recently become a five-year veteran of the agency. I am also a vice president. There are hundreds of vice presidents here; however, I am one of the few with ovaries.

Full of furtive purpose, K. and I consult the calendar like astrologers. We make decisions based on fact and instinct. We cross-reference with major and minor holidays and something exceedingly nefarious called Personal Days.

The subject of returning to work after the birth is intriguing. My reentry plan is simple thus far. I will take paid leave and unpaid leave until the people from personnel come after me with torches. Because of the extraordinary nature of you, I don't care who gets my office. I know someone will get my office, and I don't care. This is how much you signify. You are what the account planners would call a *tribe leader*.

Your father telephones from across town. Today at your father's agency, advertising involves a talking toilet that discusses its role in society with its friend the sink. A talking toilet: the bottom lip is the seat, the upper lip is the lid. The sink complains because people spit toothpaste out on him.

"Don't get me started," says the toilet.

I ask your father how it happened that one gets assigned to work on toilet products. He himself is on barbecue sauce. "I don't know," your father says, musing. "But they've written some pretty good dialogue between the sink and the toilet."

I spoke with Diana today to see how her moving day from Albuquerque went, and she said that she christened her new house in Oregon by puking Thai food into the recycling bucket. I myself was so nauseated last night I lay awake for two hours, trying not to be sick. I won, too. Instead of concentrating on the waves of sickness, I thought of blue sky. Remember this.

Earlier, I had watched *The Exorcist* on television, which was probably spectacularly unhelpful because of the projectile-vomiting scenes. Yet I couldn't help watching, due to those quick, subliminal frame manipulations where the director slips in the demon face. The movie is structured so that everything is going along as usual, when suddenly you see a white-faced red-mouthed demon screaming, and then the scene reverts to normal. It's a neat little frill that I think made some epileptics have grand mal seizures. I saw that movie in 1973 with Diana. We were thirteen and I clutched her wrist until it was raw. When the demon face happened, we screamed. Twenty-two years later, we both married for the first time.

We go through everything together. This makes us the luckiest women alive.

This afternoon was my first visit to the OB-GYN. Her name is Dr. Gray and she looks like Florence Henderson, which seems right. We sat in her mauve office, and she asked me a lot of questions about how many cats did we have and is anybody Jewish. I answered everything in a stupor and stared at the framed scalpel on her wall. I wanted to ask her about it, but guessed I should save something for later. Just so we keep the mystery going.

She asked me about any other pregnancies before you, and I said, "One."

"Any complications with the abortion?" she asked. I looked at her and smiled, thinking, What planet are you from? There was the smallest of pauses. "No," I said. None except wanting to die. This does not count as a complication.

The good news is, she informed me that since I'm tall, I am entitled to gain thirty-five pounds. I don't believe I actually will gain much weight, but I decide to go along with her for now. I will pretend, for her sake and for the free vitamin samples. Then I sat naked in the examining room for twenty minutes, with a blue paper sheet draped across my public-property body. I read a *People* article about a television-sitcom actress and how crazy in love she is with this other actor, and how she has a face-sucking oxygen machine that makes her look younger, and how she wants to lose twenty pounds. The media is deeply concerned about her weight, but she seems to be happy nonetheless, although you never know. You really can't tell how people are doing from magazine interviews.

Sitcom Actress says she fasts and that she loves to fast, that it gives her enormous clarity. I will never be able to fast, I know. Maybe that's why I don't get to be on the cover of *People* or have any clarity. But still, if she's fasting, then maybe they're going to find out that fasting backfires, judging from the recent shot of her in a Hawaiian muumuu on the cover of *The National Enquirer.* Any cover is a good cover, though. That's another truism.

Finally the doctor came in and told me to slide down the table and put my feet in the stirrups. I did what she asked. If she had said, Okay, now bark like a dog, I would have. I'd known her forty minutes and she already had my absolute trust because she has delivered twelve healthy babies to women I personally know, one of whom was forty-six. This puts Dr. Lorraine Gray right above Moses and just below Picasso in my book.

Then she said, "You're due September fourteenth. Everything should be fine." And I just thought, Huh. How she knows that from just sticking her hands up me for a minute is a David Copperfield kind of fact, and I was not going to probe further. I take my manna where I find it. When I walked outside, the January sun was shining. This seemed meaningful, I took this also.

If you ever want a baby, make love every other day. That is how you happened. You were planned, tried for, summoned. You are the closest I will ever come to magic.

I told people at work that I was pregnant. I was planning to wait until much later, but I had to explain lying on my office floor weeping to Broadway musicals.

When I told my partner, Gavin, he immediately planned to quit when I leave for maternity leave. He is loyal that way. Gavin is under thirty, has short blue hair, and looks good in anything. He is a fine-art director and knows he can always get work. Gavin and I bonded when we were both first hired, five years ago. We sensed each other immediately and began demanding to work together. Creative partners couple that way; it is much like love in the almost instantaneous way it naturally occurs.

Today I am supposed to be writing advertising copy for the sides of boxes and going to meetings about the sides of the boxes. I feel wary. If I do go to the meetings, I know I will object to something someone has done to the box, and the account people will weigh in with what they know about boxes. We will all begin to care about the boxes: my instinct is that this should be avoided. Still, the box people persist. My message light blinks spastically.

Now that I've come out as a breeding woman, I feel concern. I'm slightly worried that I won't have any authority left when I get big and have Pamela Anderson breasts. I may have to compensate in some way. I may have to start going to meetings.

Meanwhile, my olfactory senses are unreasonably intense. I can smell an orange a mile away. I can smell fear on an Oregon raccoon. I am a dog now, discerning a dozen scents at once all in bright clarity; yet I am without a dog's enthusiasm for what he is gleaning.

Last week there was a big party at work where everyone got drunk; the next day I couldn't stand next to people without gagging. They all smelled like Ted Kaczynski. They were all stumblebum, pissed-on serial killers, right down to the sweetest twenty-two-year-old secretary. This, I hope, will not last.

As with everything, there is an upside. If it turns out I am not able to work at the office because of nausea and the Ted Kaczynskis, I can contact the FDA and offer my services to locate and identify bad meat.

Despite all this, it's hard to believe that you are real. It's hard to believe that I am real. If it weren't for report cards and school pictures, it would be tempting to believe that I never was a child at all. And I know I was never as small as you are now: half an inch. I could sneeze you. It's fortunate you're inside me. If you were outside me, I would lose you. Not that you're not precious; you are, which is what would place you in terrible danger. Historically, I lose immediately that which is most precious to me. I lost a favorite pair of earrings shaped like Queen Anne shoes, and I had never lost an entire pair of earrings. You see how it is.

Why would anyone trust me with a baby?

~

Ten weeks gone.

Stayed home from work today. The queasiness is an everyday thing. Naturally I worry: if I can't handle this, how am I ever going to be a mother? I am emotionally and physically feeble.

Diana says that the first trimester is all about Fatigue, Nausea, and Paranoia.

Then your father comes home and proceeds to assemble his dinner. I had previously asked him not to cook while I was nauseated, which, like CNN, is around the clock. I hear a *hiss hiss hiss* coming from the kitchen. And it's the *pressure cooker*, releasing big jets of beet stink into the house. He's making himself a mess of beets. And I just blink at him as the house fills with the stench of it. I feel a wave of despair so great that I have to go downstairs into the bedroom and shut the door, or else I am going to pick up the pressure cooker and hurl it through the kitchen window. I imagine the thing just sailing through the air, still hissing, and the tinkly sound of the glass breaking. It is so real that I have to remove myself from the vicinity or else it is just going to happen without me.

I lie in bed and hear the *hiss hiss hiss* and try not to inhale as the air moistens and I think, This is the worst thing he has ever done to me. Death by beet. I feel he is the most ignorant man alive right now. I want to harm him in some way. I know he doesn't understand what it's like to carry you and feel sick all day and night, but that really is insignificant in the light of his crime.

I imagine a jury of pregnant women chewing on Rolaids and unanimously holding up cards that read GUILTY.

~

Today I go back to Penniman Street in West Oakland, where I lived with my mother and brother until I was twelve. The neighborhood seems a diorama of itself, small and trashy beyond comprehension. A man in a parked metallic blue Cougar waits to kill someone. Three brown faces with stained teeth laugh as I walk by a tiny backyard. No matter how shabby, every window is decorated with Christmas ornaments. Overstuffed Dumpsters festooned with maggots stand like sentinels against the crumbling apartment buildings.

We could be in any one of these houses. Why we don't have to be is a mystery.

I will keep you from this, if I can. But I think you should know it exists. I will bring you here myself when the time comes. I will show you the other side, and I hope you will feel fortunate and yet not superior. There are more good poor people than there are good rich people. Unfortunately, there are also more poor people in general. Jesus said there always would be, then he got a foot bath. You have to love Jesus.

I drive down MacArthur Boulevard to visit the public school I attended in 1970. Parking my car, I see that there are several letters missing from the sign. I see cracked pavement and broken stairs and rust-caked drinking fountains. Terrible to imagine beautiful young mouths bending to those fountains, but they do. They bend down and they drink.

I am able to enter the halls without suspicion, since those in charge have long since stopped caring what strangers pass. As I walk from classroom to classroom, the hall itself seems to lurch to one side. I place my hand inside a hole in a wall the institutional color of mold. I see the crippled desks and broken blackboards and shattered light fixtures. Slave ships are what come to mind. Bodies headed for something worse. This place I remember as fine is no longer remotely fine, is now a crumbling detention center for children too poor to escape. All of the students here are now black; the white children were airlifted to safety sometime in the eighties. These are the poor children, the children who are being thrown out.

I feel shame. Shame for being glad for you, that you will not have to come here. Shame that I cannot write a check and fix this. Shame for my late-model car and my Italian purse and my tiny cellular phone. Shame for having come from this and shame for having gotten away. There is unfairness in the world, there are atrocities that no one speaks of. We are none of us without blame.

Later I call the school. The receptionist says they are in pretty good shape, compared to the other schools. Alcatraz flits through my head, but I don't pursue it.

The principal is extremely busy, the receptionist says, but will call me back.

"What do you usually suggest to ex-students who want to help?" I ask.

"We've never had anyone call before," she says.

I feel I am transporting an ocean with an eyedropper, but I ask for their mailing address so I can write a large and terrifying check. If it doesn't scare you, it doesn't count.

Also I leave my name and phone number. "Class of seventy-three," I say, in a joking manner, but I am serious also. I am naming myself.

"Oh. Well," she says. "We don't have those records anymore."

Someday, a long time from now, you will have the feeling that the water is closing around you. It is not an altogether unpleasant sensation, growing up.

I worry. Deeply, about everything that is going on with you. I hope you're getting enough oxygen and protein and everything.

I hope you're sailing along despite my general unseemliness. I mean, I don't even *floss*. Also, I am thirty-eight years old, old enough to be your grandmother.

Your eyes have already formed, although according to the book, they look sort of double-barreled right now. Your tail is going away also. You're looking much less like something one would dip in cocktail sauce.

I have terrible fears that you have no spine, or a leg coming out of one ear. I know this is very likely untrue, but I fear these things and worse. I think of what could be wrong now, and I project ahead. In my mind you are graduating from high school with honors despite having Down's syndrome. You have your own television series, of course.

God, please help me. Please don't let what I deserve to happen, happen.

Your mother has not exactly led a pristine life. No one from the Christian channel would ever speak of me with pride, or ask for money on my behalf. I have had a life filled with important mistakes and self-destructive festivals that lasted years. Although at this point in my life, I am somewhat boring; my most subversive act now is to return audio materials into the BOOKS ONLY slot at the library. Age has slowed me down.

Every morning I wake up between four and five A.M. with a gnawing sensation deep in my stomach. At this point I have to get up, go upstairs into the icy-floored kitchen, eat a bowl of cereal, and then go back to bed. And then hours later, when I wake up for good, I need to pour another bowl. Slop the hogs.

In the cupboard I have Wheat Chex, Rice Chex, Froot Loops, Spoon Size Shredded Wheat, Sugar Smacks, Corn Chex, Product

19, and Raisin Bran. Soon I must go and replenish these with new cereals, because I am becoming immune to all eight. Sliced bananas help, but they are losing their power, too.

It's you. You're a parasite. I told a coworker this, and she said, "Oh no. You have to stop calling the baby that." I tried to explain that you couldn't hear me yet, that your ears were decorative at this juncture, but she still looked at me like I was Joseph Stalin. For this reason I won't call you a parasite anymore. It's not up to you, I know you are under strict biological orders to double your size every week and that this takes a lot of fodder, but I do wish you'd pace yourself in a more considerate fashion.

Tonight I listened to your father eat dinner while I sat in another room. I can't enjoy my food; nor can I stand the aroma of others eating. But I could hear him. Every saliva-ridden mouthful, every bite, every chew. He wasn't even trying to be discreet. He ate with a horrible gusto.

It's good that divorce lawyers don't magically appear at such times, like Satan with Dr. Faust. I would definitely sign. I would sign and then laugh long and maniacally as the black Hades Express Toboggan pulled up outside our front door.

The problem is being so hyperaware. Just when you get pregnant and you really need to be medicated, you are denied all medication, even aspirin. I feel flayed, skinless. Oversober. I miss the highs and lows of drinking and smoking and light pharmaceuticals. I feel like the only one who didn't get the 3-D glasses for the disaster movie. Meanwhile, your father has a big frosty martini after work, with two garlic-stuffed olives.

Up until a few weeks ago, I was doing all right eating Hostess chocolate cupcakes and mayonnaisey sandwiches, making that my cross-addiction, but suddenly all food seems verboten. I guess it's important that all brand new potential mothers be forbidden the least little pleasure, that they be crushed completely by the wheel of life.

It's not your fault. You're just a little baby. Not even a baby, you haven't reached that status yet. According to the books, you're not even a fetus. An embryo is what you are. It sounds scary and test-tube-like and diminutive: *embryo*. God, they slap you with the titles already, and you're not even born.

I scheduled myself for a CVS test instead of an amniocentesis. This is a relatively new procedure in which the doctor extracts a sample of chorionic villus tissue from the womb. These bits of tissue hold all your information; they form the Ouija board of your destiny. But then today I read in one very pessimistic medical book that the risks of CVS may outweigh the benefits. There is also a rumored association between CVS and limb deformity: like, one of your arms could become a fin. The theme song from *Flipper* is stuck in my brain right now; it's bad.

They call him Flipper, Flipper
Faster than lightning . . .

Then I read the other six books, which didn't seem as dire, but they all admitted that the CVS has slightly higher risks for miscarriage than the amnio. So now I feel like a killer, even though the test is ten days away. I feel like I've already killed you. The police are on their way.

The benefit is that with the CVS, I would know everything about you in your eleventh week instead of your seventeenth. So if you're not okay, or I have an ectopic pregnancy and you need to jettison the pod, so to speak, it can happen a lot sooner. This involves a horrid decision that we must not even consider. The word *terminate* is what they use. It sounds like I'd be firing you, but it's not like that. I'd be allowing you to leave a bad house. If my pipes have burst and my foundation is shot, then I'll know it, and you can just take off. I'd want you to.

Would your soul survive, is the question some people would ask. I know so.

Besides, sometimes you have to cut your losses, and I think even an embryo understands that, and your tiny baby-soul self would just move on to greener pastures. You're not like me, a thirty-eight-year-old Buick in need of repair. You're fresh from the place where everything waits to be born, and I think you would just turn around and go back until another opportunity arose. You'd rise up and move on. Meanwhile, I'd be stuck back here in this *high-risk* body with my brain of Fiddle-Faddle and dirt, and my guilt and dreams of trains crashing.

The truth is, I can't even think of it, termination, without my mind folding over on itself. Already it is like imagining my own death, only worse, because I would be conscious. I don't see myself as brave and philosophical, I see myself swan-diving off the roof.

I want the other pregnancy. The one without risks or spina bifida. The twenty-two-year-old's pregnancy. That's the best age to have a baby. Twenty-two. I couldn't even drive a clutch at twenty-two. I don't understand the whole fascistic, ageist system, except I know now that I have misplanned my life and there are severe penalties being extracted. The threat of termination and limb deformity has been wielded. Everyone says "Don't worry" and "Oh, you'll be fine," but they don't KNOW. No one knows. Only you know, and you are the soul of discretion.

What should I do? Should I have the CVS? Blink once for yes and twice for no.

This is how I know that the soul survives beyond death. I will tell you.

When I was thirty, I was speaking with an attractive man, and I said, "My father marched with Martin Luther King." At the time I felt a secret shame, because it seemed like the worst sort of name-dropping, to talk about two people who were dead and then cobble it into a self-esteem boost. But I did it, and the man was duly impressed.

A few weeks later I was on the phone with Diana, whose father was dying of cancer, and then a couple of minutes later I mentioned that my father had marched with Martin Luther King. I did it again. Catapulting off a dying man, no less. And this time, instead of just a tinge of shame, I felt a wave of revulsion. Because it wasn't a fact, it was something my mother had alluded to in passing, and my mother has never been a slave to the truth. Doubtless she made it up so that I would have something to feel proud of, despite my father's being a frequently unemployed alcoholic who died with the IRS hot on his trail and a bag of empty Popov bottles below the sink. And so, at that moment, on the phone to Diana, I promised myself that I would never again tell people this. I shut it out of my mind and decided that I would have to get along without that little piece of folklore. This was on a Tuesday.

The next day I am about to leave work and my mother calls me. She says, "Do you remember Mrs. Ebling from the church? Well, after forty-six years, she's selling her house and she came across something I think you might like to have." And I say, "Okay, whatever. I'll stop by and pick it up tonight on my way home." She hangs up.

I arrive at my mother's house. I walk into the kitchen and she says, "Here," and hands me a letter. It is a letter dated 1965, type-written on stationery from the First Baptist Church on Eureka

Street, the ministry where my father used to preach before he found booze and San Francisco and left home for higher ground. It's a letter documenting that my father was selected to attend Dr. Martin Luther King's Freedom March on Selma, Alabama. I am so shocked I just fold it up and say, "Thanks," and walk out of the kitchen and get into my car. All the way home, tears blind me.

And I think of my father, Richard, way up in heaven, pulling all those infinitesimal strings so that the letter gets into my hands on that particular Wednesday. He waited only one day, so that I would be certain, and probably also because he always had a high sense of drama and apparently those qualities stay with a person even when they move on. He had no voice to speak with, as when he was a minister, but he could still move earthly things; he could prove something.

It was his way of saying, I'm here, and I'm fine. And you are, too.

Your grandfather was a good man. He went wrong on a lot of things, but he was also pure of heart, and he would want you to believe in something. I hope you will.

It was Dr. King who said, "The arc of universal truth is long, but it bends towards justice."

Your father got up at four A.M. last night and ate a bowl of cereal with me. I had Rice Chex, he had Wheat Chex. He seems to be gaining a little weight, and it's just sad. I myself look like a swimsuit model.

You can't see yet, so I will tell you what I look like. I am six feet tall, with cheekbones like Sophia Loren's and no hips to speak of. I have long honey-blond hair past my waist and the whitest teeth you can imagine. My eyes are the color of sapphires. My features are what they call *classical*. Every day men drive onto the sidewalk craning their necks to get a glimpse of me, but I walk on. I walk like Uma Thurman and I have double eyelashes. People are jealous of my looks, and that has caused me a great deal of pain all my life, but what can you expect. Right now the bushes around our house are filled with people from fashion magazines, waiting to get a glimpse of me and see what fashion trends will be upcoming for fall. (Actually, I'm a 5'8" brunette, and we have no bushes. We couldn't keep bushes alive. What does that say to you, you may well ask.)

Here in bed, I am dressed in a tattered U.C. Berkeley T-shirt and a pair of your father's boxer shorts, surrounded by my bibles. They are: *The Mayo Clinic Complete Book of Pregnancy, The Columbia University College of Physicians and Surgeons Guide to Pregnancy, Having a Baby: A Complete Guide for the Mother-to-Be, What to Expect When You're Expecting, The Complete Book of Pregnancy and Childbirth* by Sheila Kitzinger, *The Girlfriends' Guide to Pregnancy,* and *A Child Is Born*, which is mostly photographs. Whenever I have a question, I look up the answer in each book, which all have conflicting information and wildly divergent facts, and then I listen to the answer that I like best.

Having a Baby is particularly good because it was published in the sixties and it talks about being able to pop pills and chain- smoke with nary a repercussion. It includes a diary of a young mother, with excerpts such as "September 18, John and Pat came over for dinner. Had a double whiskey to celebrate John's raise." Then there are medical footnotes in the margin that say, "There is no reason to believe that moderate drinking should harm your baby in any way."

Then my friend who has never had a baby calls me up and says, "Have you heard about the tap-water thing?"

"What about it?" I say.

"Causing miscarriages," she says.

"What tap water?" I say. My head is beginning to pound.

"I don't know. It could be in Berkeley or it could be all over," she says. "I only caught the end of the news."

"Oh," I say. "Great."

"I thought hundreds of people would have told you by now," she says.

"No," I say. Not only am I going to miscarry, but I am bereft of people to tell me the news. I'm screwed, you're screwed, and we have no informed friends.

"Well," I say. "I guess I'll go kill myself now." And then I hang up and try to call my OB-GYN's office, but it's twelve-thirty and they are all at lunch. Probably celebrating the tap water thing, planning their free time and laughing gaily over bottles of fine wine. Saying, "Do you think we should tell them? Naaaaah."

Finally I call Marin Water, and the woman tells me about the chemical they've been studying, it's in water and it's called trihalomethane. She explains that the report hasn't even been *released* yet. I'm like, Whew. Well then, it must not be true, right? Uh-huh.

Then she says the report was based on a level of seventy-five, and ours is only fifty. Plus, it helps to boil the water, or to use a water filter for drinking water (we do). She says she thinks that actually, people getting scared and worrying might be what's causing the trouble.

"Yes," I say. "But you don't miscarry from worrying."

"No," she says. "Of course not."

I wonder what size tap shoes she wears. She sounds petite, so maybe six, six and a half. I'm sure the bottled-springwater truck is pulling right the fuck up to her house every Thursday, but I don't say this. I say, and this is weird, I actually say, "Thank you," and hang up.

Thank you for trihalomethane.

What will I be after you are born?

If I leave my job while you are nursing, I will no longer be a creative director. Nor will I be a vice president. All of my hard-earned and obsessed-over titles will fall around my ankles. This makes me feel, as I consider it, unclothed.

It's what Gloria Steinem is referring to when she says, "Women make themselves real by doing."

Even if I return to work, I will be vaguely disrespected by some of the people in my profession. To them I will seem tamed, domestic, stuffed into a chintz pigeonhole. Lesser.

I worry that I will become nothing at all. I worry that I will become, by strict definition, a mommy. This is a wonderful thing to be and, it strikes me, a terrible thing to be. For any woman.

I resolve to remain a person, and not to be sucked into a place from which I am unable to return. The place where so many women go and are never seen again.

I do this not just for me but for you. There will be no mother blood on your hands.

God works in mysterious ways, baby, and there is never more evidence of this than when your life is going along fairly well, actually sailing. The sensation of wind through your hair becomes, for an extremely brief time, commonplace. It is then that God lowers the cosmic boom. He will not show up; that is the kind view. The unkind view is that he sits back to watch with a highball and a bowl of nuts.

My friend Elaine keeps a file folder that she has labeled His Miracles to Perform. She keeps the file full of newspaper clippings from around the world. Here are two stories she recently relayed from her file.

One was about a small child who reached down into the shimmering baptismal water at a beautiful Catholic altar. When he reached into the holy water, the whole structure came crashing down, killing him instantly.

"His mysterious ways," Elaine said, in a deadpan murmur.

The second story Elaine told me from His Miracles to Perform was about a mother in a tiny Mexican village who made sugar cookies for her seven relatives. They all died.

The Mexican authorities came in to investigate and pronounced: It was the flour.

All the flour was disposed of.

Later that week, the same woman had a wake for her relatives. Twenty-six people attended from all corners of the village. Everyone died.

The authorities came back and examined everything again.

We were wrong, they said. It was the *sugar.*

Today I am at the dentist getting my teeth cleaned, and the new hygienist tells me the pockets are getting deeper toward the back molars. As she says this, she offers a thumbs-down. Her teeth are perfect. I would like her to be fried, along with some new potatoes. I have approximately three original factory teeth left.

From behind her rubber gloves and her bright green plastic visor and her surgical mask, she asks me, "Have you heard about pregnancy gingivitis?"

"Yes," I say in a happy and excited tone of voice. "I'm really looking forward to it."

I hope this will keep her from further conversation, and it does. Have you heard about pregnancy schizophrenia, in other words.

This did not, however, stay her from her appointed rounds. There were four instruments employed. An electric drill, a long pointy stick, a hooked spike, and a nozzle that sprayed icy water.

My mouth feels as though I have been chewing razor blades, the teeth loose as dice. This must be very good for me, this procedure. As I leave, I make my next cleaning appointment, in four months' time. I smile the smile of the damned. The gum losers.

When I get back to my office, I call my periodontist. I can hear him rubbing his hands together and speed-dialing the Porsche dealership. But there is nothing to be done. These are my gums. There is no escaping them.

Your grandfather Richard had bad gums, but he died at forty-four. He had a way of getting around things.

Your father has excellent gums. So your chances are about fifty-fifty. I am sorry for this, but there is nothing I can do about it now.

Upon reflection, perhaps what you should do is get your baby teeth first, lose your baby teeth, get your adult teeth, and then start thinking about gums. Really, you've got enough to do, growing a nose.

Your grandfather Richard was born in Minnesota in 1935. He had a brother named Charles, who was younger and worshiped him. His parents were named Fern and Don, and they were church-going people, the kind of quiet country people who talk about what they will have for lunch while they're eating breakfast.

Richard died in an automobile accident. Actually, there were two accidents—one where his car was sideswiped and rolled over, and another one that happened a minute later. While Richard stood by the car waiting for help, another car came along and hit him. He knew nothing, and for that I am glad. I wouldn't want him to suffer, and if that means flying through the air at high speed, then so be it.

Please, never stand in the middle of a freeway.

As a child, I saw my paternal grandparents as tall people who mustn't be annoyed. I tried to be quiet. They always seemed old to me. Fern used to bake elaborate cookies with me, but then later on she was confined to a wheelchair by multiple sclerosis. After my parents divorced, we never saw my grandparents, except for one trip in 1967 when my parents pretended they were normal even though they weren't, they were already broken. I learned about appearances from that trip. We all got new clothes and acted happy. When we came back, my father left home. I don't remember what happened right after that.

Until recently, I had never seen a picture of my father as a child. I wrote to his brother, Charles, and asked if there were any photos. I received a box full of old black-and-white pictures. I saw Richard revealed as a pale, spectacled boy with a newspaper bag slung over his shoulder. He is thin and wan and looks secretive. You can already see he is holding things back for later. He is planning to get out of Minnesota and do wrong.

He has sent me big messages from beyond but not many. Mostly he has stayed away. He could be doing incredible, fantastic things on the other side, making sure parents smell a fire starting in the living room, helping kitty cats off roofs. He may be. He is not really helping me, but then I don't know that for sure.

We had nineteen years together. He didn't start drinking until I was six; that's six relatively perfect years. They say the character is formed by age five, so for that I am grateful. I am. You take what you get, is my experience, and run like mad.

I remember him carrying me on his shoulders, remember him telling me I was a good artist. I liked to paint then. I don't anymore. Now I write, it's all I can do, and there are days when I question that, too, but I go on.

Life is grotesquely uncertain, but there is one thing that will never change: I love you. This I iron-clad guarantee. When I die, I want you to know that I will always try to be available in case of emergency. I will hover like the scent of stargazer lilies. And someday, when you die, I will come to meet you and make sure you find your way around.

I will escort you into death as I escorted you into life. I will have that privilege.

I couldn't do any work today at the agency. *Why* am I so tired, I ask myself. Then I remember that I am making a person.

This entire week has pretty much been a blank. I shuffle books around and put Post-its indiscriminately on documents and the pages of magazines. I surf the Internet with a false aura of purpose. I know I will work again, but I am in no hurry. Everything seems much slower now.

Generally, when you can't work, it is because you have somehow used up what fodder resides in your brain. There are those that remain empty always and never actually create anything. I'm not sure that's a goal; the boredom alone would annihilate your spirit. Yet it could be splendid, being empty. You could become a great spiritual leader, or an executive producer.

One more thing I know: no matter what, don't ever join the music clubs that offer to send you ten free.

El Niño. The rain keeps coming. People's houses are falling downhill. The Pacific coast is sweeping away couples in love, couples who visit the brink of the surf to admire nature's majesty and end up screaming in thin air. Two were lost yesterday. Gone.

I'm lying in bed eating unseasoned Ry-Krisp. It's 10:53 A.M. on a Saturday and I feel sad. I think this is a mood swing, but it doesn't feel like a swing. It feels like a plunge. Down, down.

Meanwhile, your father smells like garbage. He used to smell fine, but somehow now he smells exactly like the back of a Chinese restaurant, midweek. I am puzzled as to what line of action I should take.

My doctor says that it's probably me, that women in their first trimester can smell things, including body odors, more acutely, and that it passes, but she doesn't know when. I feel bereft. I have been robbed of your father. I can't be near him, or else I feel I will gag. I thought it was from alcohol, so I asked him to stop drinking, and he has, mostly. But still the garbage smell wafts off his body, so I can't hug him or sleep next to him.

I am wretched. This is some further punishment from the gods, being extracted for sins I have obviously forgotten but the gods have not. Oh yes, their mills grind exceedingly fine. My best friend and only comfort, your father, has been turned into a Dumpster with legs. I've asked him to forgo both garlic and onions, but he does them behind my back, as though he's going to the electric chair and can never have them again. I hugged him last night and he held his breath. He thinks it's on his breath, the odor, but actually it's everywhere. I asked him what he was doing. "I'm holding my breath," he said, in a strangled voice. I find this so touching.

Spent the last three nights curled up in a comforter on the futon. Pregnancy quarantine.

Your father says I should keep a bag of peanuts in my car so that I never get too hungry. This seems to me a sensible idea. Getting hungry is when the nausea happens, and the fatigue. My blood sugar dips like mad. I am a deep-sea blood-sugar diver and have to watch out for the gastric bends.

So now I have a can of Planters cocktail peanuts in my car. It feels like the bit of extra security I have been looking for. Each morning I nibble a few on my way to the ad agency, and again on the way home. I am also drinking my weight in Calistoga water. The bubbles are good for my nausea but bad for my gas. What I should name you is Flatulence. Or Flatula. That's pretty.

In the first trimester you can't win, you can only keep from driving into a rail.

So far your name has been Zoe, Pablo, Gigi, Jules, Pascale, and the current favorite, Sabine.

I dream I am stretched out on the examining table having the CVS, and a nurse says, "There's something wrong." One of the nurses is white, the other one, the one in charge, is black and impassive. She snaps off a rubber glove and walks on thick-soled silent shoes toward the back of the room, flipping a switch. The lights flicker but then come back on. I want to say something but I can't, my voice doesn't work in the dream. The machines keep whirring, and the nurses' eyes are dark holes above the white surgical masks. And everything is very quiet, and there is no one there with me except the nurses, who have gone completely silent as if to say, I'm so sorry.

When I tell your father about this dream, he is already dressed for work. He sits on the edge of the bed, stroking my stomach with his right hand, drinking coffee with his left.

Your father doesn't smell like garbage anymore, he has his regular smell back. I can stretch my body out alongside his again at night and read under his arm. This is fantastic news. One for our side.

~

We leave in half an hour for the CVS test. Last night was an exercise in terror. Crying, thrashing, thinking about all the what-ifs. The first thing they're going to do is perform a sonogram *to make sure the baby's alive.* That one phrase, which I read in a book last night at ten P.M., was enough to send me cartwheeling into blackness.

You're probably not even concerned. Just kicking back in your own piss, making toenails.

Your father minimizes my fears, but he doesn't have a clue. The planet he is on is so far from the planet I am on, you can't even send messages. We're both tense, although he won't admit it. Recently he stormed out of the bedroom over a matter of little importance. But a while later, he came back and held me. I listened to him snoring, and that seemed marginally better than being alone. A mate buffers.

Slept fitfully. Dreamed I was a vampire witch and could fly. And had the ability to stop time for everyone except me and the person I wanted to be alone in time with.

In three and a half hours it will all be over. I hope that you are alive, I pray that you are alive.

Irrationally, I think of logistical things: I've already ordered a subscription to *Hip Mama* magazine, including back-ordered #5: Special Nervous Breakdown Issue. I have also bought a plane ticket for Diana to fly out from Portland to San Francisco on March 12, for the Pregnant Women's Getaway Tour.

When your father and I were in Paris on our honeymoon, we had matching hats made that said *Lune de Miel '96*. This is French for Honeymoon '96.

I love both of you so much I may explode. Cream of Wheat everywhere.

Please, please, please.

We walked into the perinatal testing office and a woman with long dark hair and a purple suit told us about the genetic testing we were about to undergo. She showed us the chart of forty-two normal chromosome pairs, and then she showed us the undesirable chromosomes. The extra chromosomes, the ill-numbered chromosomes. The chromosomes of doom.

I wish she hadn't shown them to me. I am very suggestible and may subconsciously rearrange chromosomes by mistake. Anything seemed possible in that place; that place exists to expose possibilities. The maternal age charts revealed that you have a one in twelve chance of being born with some sort of genetic irregularity. This is much worse than what the books said. My hands feel numb.

She spoke very quickly and precisely and yet with warmth and reassurance. Her name is Judith, and she is holding all the cards.

It took forty-five minutes to hear everything Judith had to say, and near the end, I actually yawned, which made me feel guilty, like God will see that and say, Oh, she's not paying attention? Well, I know how to fix *that*.

Then they gave me this big clear plastic cup of water with a straw and said my bladder had to be full in order for the sonogram to function, and so I drank the water. I wanted to ask if it was tap water, but at that point it seemed moot. If I have the extra chromosomes, they're already slam-dancing their way to chaos.

We went into the examining room and I of course started balking and saying, "I'm scared," but your father rubbed my neck and helped me tie the back of my hospital gown. One in twelve, baby. One in twelve.

The sonogram screen was all set up with my name at the top, and that was fascinating; there was a pie-shaped black space where your image was going to appear, and I got excited but also very worried. Voyage to the Bottom of the Uterus.

I lay back on the examining table, and then a woman came in to give me the sonogram. And the whole time I'm praying, Please don't let it be a black nurse and a white nurse, like in my dream. And it wasn't, it was a single young nurse, and she squirted gel on my stomach; they had warmed the gel, which provided a small, ineffable comfort. Then she placed the electric-shaver receptor on my belly and turned on the machine, and there was static on the screen and I watched with all my attention, anxious to see you and see that you are all right. But I couldn't tell yet, it just all looked like a snowstorm on Mars. And the nurse was frowning ever so slightly and adjusting the machine and this seemed the longest moment ever, a moment when people are born and live and die, and then she finally said, "There's the body, there's the head." And I asked in this tremulous voice, "Is the heart beating?" And she said, "Yes."

I began to cry, and then the picture went haywire because when my stomach moved we couldn't see you. So I stopped, and she handed me a tissue from a box right on top of the machine. This is a delicate business, and they are prepared for the worst sort of cowards and emotional cripples like your mom.

And there you were, this little white curly shape on the screen, tiny and suspended inside a vast heart-shaped darkness. You were just a coffee bean of life. There was a minute pulsing mark in your center, and that was your heart beating, very fast like a bird. Your father saw it first. "There's the heartbeat," he said, squeezing my hand. He seemed excited, as though he was watching a ball game on which he had money. Then you suddenly did one dramatic act: you moved. You adjusted yourself and then you were still again, I almost thought it didn't happen, but your father pointed to the screen and said, "Look!" A high fly to deep left.

Relief and wonder were flooding my brain, and then the other doctor, the CVS specialist, came in and shook my hand and said, "It's nice to meet you."

"It's nice to meet you, too," I said. I have gotten this far; there is a heartbeat. I am getting through this in small stages. Moment by moment and day by day and procedure by procedure. I scooted down on the table, almost eagerly. I put my feet in the stirrups.

Next a long thin tube was inserted in me and through the cervix and as my uterus contracted, the sonogram screen kind of flipped and I got scared, but they said it was normal, so I took a deep breath. There was a small amount of cramping pain. Someone was strip-mining a wad of tissue from inside my uterus, but I could take it, so long as those crazy chromosomes didn't show up with their tongue studs and engineer boots.

You didn't seem to mind any of this. You stayed curled on your stomach.

Then they had enough of a sample, so they said, "That's it, it's over." They displayed the tube filled with pink liquid and tiny, algaelike white tissue. They held it right up to my eyes. They let me watch them label it.

Seven to twelve days until the results come back.

Your father helped me get dressed, like this very jolly butler. When I went to the bathroom, there was the smallest amount of light pink spotting, but they told me to expect that. I'm not supposed to worry unless it's bright red and there's lots of it, so I won't.

A few minutes later, when we left the hospital arm in arm, the sun was shining. I love your father enormously, but for the first time, something had come between us.

The moment I saw you on that screen, I began a long fall. When you moved, I felt squeezed with a wild infatuation and protectiveness. We are one. Nothing, not even death, can change that.

There's something else.

Yesterday, when I got up from the table after the CVS, there was a dark stain from the iodine solution they had swabbed my cervix with: a dark swath marring the crisp white tissue lining of the examining table. I now realize where I have seen this brown iodine before. It was when I was twenty-one. This same brown iodine was smeared on the blue paper gown I discarded when I was getting dressed to go meet my boyfriend outside Kaiser Hospital in Oakland. My mind wouldn't allow this fact in until now. It protected me, but then the protection gave out and I remembered.

I know my decision may seem rash and inhumane, especially to one in your position. The thought of someone vacuuming you out like an errant dust ball is unthinkable. I was a different person then. I was unformed. My boyfriend was a very young and almost handsome compulsive gambler who adored cocaine and liked me a lot. My father had just died and I was, I think, trying to replace him, but I couldn't go through with it.

The way I did it was by drinking a lot of alcohol and not thinking about it, by never allowing the baby to exist in my mind; also by blending in with all the other women I knew who had abortions, sometimes more than one. It was the 1980s, Reagan was president. A lot of bad shit went down.

These are all excuses. Forgive me. I have the memory to punish me, the shadow child who would now be seventeen. Your almost brother. Your almost sister.

There is nothing I can do about this. This is what is termed, in the world, a regret.

~

Your aunt Diana got her amnio results back today. A healthy boy. She's a full week ahead of me in getting her test results. She is the brave tribe member who goes into unknown territory and then returns to tell the others.

You're no longer an embryo but a fetus, by the way. Judith said so. The books say twelve weeks, but in real life they have moved you up.

My nausea has subsided a bit, with the help of Sea-Bands. These are small blue wrist bands that utilize the science of acupressure. They apply tension to the insides of your wrists, and they work. Eight dollars at any drugstore. I can't believe they don't hand out Sea-Bands to every pregnant woman, but that would be helpful, and the medical profession is understandably busy in other more vital areas, like whipping up the next batch of thalidomide. Additionally, there is the much needed research money they spent calculating the exact odds for an abnormal baby, and how those odds quadruple every two seconds after your thirtieth birthday. They have so very much to do, it's a wonder any babies get born at all.

One nice scientific advancement is the sonogram. A sonogram is live interior TV from which you can take pictures, frame grabs. I especially love your first picture, your sonogram. I carry it with me everywhere, like an inhaler.

On the picture appear the words HEAD and BODY, which the technician typed in the appropriate locations just above your image on the screen. She printed out two pictures, one with HEAD, BODY and one plain. In the sonogram picture, my uterus looks perfectly heart-shaped. A trick of the light.

At the agency, Gavin makes a sepia copy of your sonogram, messes around with it in Photoshop for about two hours, blows it up to forty times its original size, mounts it, and presents it to me. As he does this, he is listening to a bootlegged electronica dance mix of traditional German folk songs.

Gavin has blocked out all the letters save for my last name. I notice, as though for the first time, my father's last name, the one I've somehow kept.

It's like John Lee Hooker says: "He gone, but he ain't gone."

Today is Day Nine of waiting for the test results. I was doing great up until today. I was a debutante at a cotillion. I was a tall white man at the bank where he is known by name.

But today I woke up and decided that really it would be a good idea to call Judith, the woman with the purple suit. Judith is my genetic counselor, which sounds like you and I already have a crippling problem.

When I got hold of Judith on the second phone call, she sounded less pleasant than she was at the genetic-counseling interview. Much, much less pleasant. I had needlessly interrupted her in the middle of something important, her tone of voice implied. I was the five-year-old on the long car trip asking to go to the bathroom when I should have said I needed to go before.

"It's Day Nine," I said. There was a long silence.

"And, you know, I'm getting anxious."

I'm not sure why I needed to say this to another woman.

"Yessssss . . . ?"she said on a drawn-out schoolteacher note. It was not a question. It was the beginning of a sentence that is "Yes, you *are* a paranoid imbecile."

"You said I could call you if I had any questions," I said. Shame was wrestling with anger, I ignored them both: I need this person. I said nothing and waited.

After a moment she took pity on me and spilled her genetic beans. "No news is good news," she said, clearly annoyed.

She explained how she usually hears something by now if there's a problem. "They're very fast then," she said. Leading me to think, erroneously I hope, of a gaggle of white-coated sadists running to the phone like twelve-year-olds, waving the crazy chromosomes high above their heads.

She went on to say that although she had called women with normal results on Day Seven, she has also definitely made that same call at Day Fourteen.

I didn't even know there was a Day Fourteen. I felt horrified, like I was seeing my father's penis. I asked her, "You mean it's seven to fourteen days?"

"I told you: seven to fifteen days," she said. This didn't make sense, but she was quite firm. Wondering, I'm sure, why I can't just wait the allotted days and keep still. Maybe because the zombie life-suckers didn't come to my house, I wanted to say. *You insensitive professional* was also on the tip of my tongue. I didn't say this when I wanted to, early on in the conversation. Like, the first five seconds. I didn't say this, so I received *No news is good news* as my reward. (There is almost always a reward for not losing your temper. Unfortunately, there sometimes is a reward for *losing* your temper, for standing up when they are smashing you down into your given chair. It will be your job to determine which is which at each individual breaking point.)

I'm typing at seventy words per minute. The movement is keeping me from going insane.

"Bad bongos" is what your father would say.

Day Ten. I am having a hard time. I think I'm actually molting.

No news is good news doesn't seem to help as much as it should; now I am afraid that they won't call and afraid that they will. If no news is truly good news, then I should have asked the Judith woman never to call.

The phone sits silent as a religious altar. As a scaffold.

I am driving in my car and my cell phone rings. I know it is Judith with the test results.

She says, "Well, it turns out you do have fast-growing cells." Her voice is upbeat and happy, so I know. I know that you are sound, that the crazy chromosomes have not gotten you. They are moving on to a party in the Haight, and God has decided to spare me the fate I probably deserve.

Then she says that the chromosomes are all growing fine, that there is the proper amount and that the test for spina bifida came back negative, as did the Tay-Sachs; the Down's syndrome chromosomes are not in evidence.

"Thank God," I say. And I do. I am driving down Bay Street, and I can see the Golden Gate Bridge and everything. I am driving toward home.

And the next thing she says is, "And they are definitely little-boy chromosomes."

~

Two days have passed since that phone call. I haven't been able to write to you. There is something I am deeply ashamed of, so I have kept silent until now.

It was as though suddenly you unveiled, you made yourself known to me. You are a clever child, a master of deception. You are the Houdini of fetuses. Because, baby? Everyone thought you were going to be a girl. Me, your father, your grandmother, Diana, Elaine, the Chinese calendars, everybody. Even the tea-leaf reader at Chai Teahouse in Larkspur said if you were a boy, she would fall off her chair. I am going to visit her soon to see if she does.

I have to admit something to you now. For the past couple of days, I have been wrestling with a terrible, shameful feeling. This feeling came right on the heels of joy and huge relief that you were all right. It came about two seconds after that.

You see, you are to be our only child. And I have always wanted a girl, I had the hallowed girl names all picked out. I saw myself downloading all my feminine information on to you, passing it along like a very ornate bejeweled baton. I saw myself instructing you on hair, makeup, clothes, and later, if you were quick, accessories. You were going to be my little girlfriend, my companion in the mysterious dance of yin. And in the moment I knew you were going to go your own inexorable way, I experienced a loss.

It gets worse.

I was going to create you in my own image. You were, I think, going to be me; only younger, with your soul intact and not cracked and edgy like mine. You were to be my avenging angel, my new self all fresh and shiny and unspoiled, ready to go forth into the world and make things right. I had your bags all packed. I was an out-of-control bus careening toward the gully of resurrection. I see that now.

43

That night, after happily announcing your sex to everyone, I wept. I am thirty-eight, and know now that I will never have a daughter. A daughter is a precious and secret dream I have carried with me since I was five. Your father heard me crying and said I was crazy, and that he had no sympathy for me. He said I was hurting his feelings because, lest I forget, he was a boy, too. How could I be so ungrateful? I had no answer except the wind rushing past my ears as I fell down the chasm of self-loathing.

But baby, what I need you to understand right here and now is, it wasn't about you at all. I wasn't upset because I was having a boy. I was upset that I wasn't having a girl and in all likelihood never would. Perhaps as a woman I was, in some hideously final sense, finished. I don't expect you to understand this, but you seem very wise and agile, so I hope you will try. Because, baby, there is news. I have spoken with the Voice.

I should explain the Voice. I am as far from religious as it is possible to be in San Francisco. I laugh openly at television evangelists and consider Oral Roberts the worst sort of predator. Yet I am the daughter of a minister turned bartender, so I have a kind of foxhole faith that lives inside me, and I found it that night. I heard the Voice, coming from inside or above. It doesn't matter.

Voice said that the door for such things was, until further notice, ajar. And that this was something I couldn't control, life. This was news to me. I had conceived exactly on schedule, passed all my tests. I am a vice president at a major ad agency. I assumed I could executive-produce. In my wild arrogance, I thought I was controlling not only conception and life but gender.

Voice explained that He/She had the keys to the van. The best thing Voice said was that I get to be reborn as a man. That part of me is in you, and I will experience something many women never get to.

Voice said that maybe I was not finished, but maybe I was. Voice stressed that no mistakes were ever made where these things are decided. None. It wasn't like the government. And that having a boy was exactly what my soul needed most.

The next morning I went into the bedroom and lay with your father and said that everything was fine. I told him about the Voice, and that we had struck a deal. And your father believed me, although I wasn't fool enough to disclose all the particulars. Your father trusts me more than I do myself.

I see now that, besides you, the real gift was discovering something important inside of me. Extracting a lump of bias that I never knew existed. Over time it could have grown and become something else, something twisted and more damaging. Something that I fear I could have unwittingly passed along, had you been a girl. But you would not allow that.

Thank you for being a boy. You are already teaching me. I feel contrite and small, yet I contain everything. You.

Feeling so good these days I have to marvel. There was that six-week vomity Epstein-Barr thing, and then you settled yourself and my systems shifted back.

Tomorrow is the last day of my first trimester, so this is all on schedule, the lessening of early symptoms. You have a touching sense of punctuality, as well as the quality of mercy. I feel somehow that you are kind and do not wish me to suffer. I guess we'll know whether I am right about this when the time comes to push you out.

At this point you are in favor only of cold-filtered water from the Britta dispenser in the refrigerator. I have completely lost my taste for sodas or coffee. Conversely, I get so high swigging an Odwalla Strawberry C Monster that I feel guilty and can only drink half. This is your method, to have me crave what you want, and to eschew what you don't. You have assumed almost full power. You won't abide nicotine, alcohol, margarine, or chicken fat. You're like this very strict Mormon vegan.

The question *Who am I?* seems pertinent, although I must say you are doing a much better job with my diet and life than I have done in the past. However, I feel you have some control issues that we may need to confront at a later time.

Twelve weeks gone.

I had a little spotting this morning, and it made my heart stop. I read in my bibles that sometimes this happens on the day a woman would have gotten her period. I checked the calendar, and sure enough: this is the day my third missed period would have arrived had you not made your entrance. I took to my bed for the weekend, a dog of terror at my heels. It once again made me realize how much I am subsumed into you. There can be no *no* you, as far as I am concerned. It would be unacceptable.

My thirty-ninth birthday. After two solid months of rain, it was sunny and warm. I have convinced myself that you control sun. The official term for this is *pathetic fallacy*.

Your father took me out to a lavish breakfast. At the restaurant, I had the quintessential eggs Benedict, the eggs Benedict

to which all other eggs Benedicts aspire. The secret is pepper bis-
cuit and no ham, which I had them leave out because it felt threatening. The potatoes on the side were thinly sliced and made a
sublime conductor for the hollandaise sauce. I was moaning
through the whole dish.

Then the piano player began his set with "Call Me Irrespon-
sible," which was your grandfather's favorite song. It was a rather
embarrassingly obvious message, typical of him and especially poi-
gnant because it's my birthday.

I'm irresponsibly mad about you . . .

Where people inevitably flounder is by not making sure there is
enough banana in the banana split. I made two for your father
and me tonight, with the perfect amount of banana (one whole
each) and the kind of whipped cream that squirts out of a can. As
I shot the whipped cream, I felt a sharp urge to laugh out loud, so
I did.

Your father calls all this a *craving*. I will allow him to believe
this because it benefits me to do so. In truth, I've never stopped
wanting a banana split every day since I was twelve years old and
senselessly gave them up. Now I feel entitled. I am experiencing
a wave of power, that seems primarily connected to butterfat,
cream, and whole-egg mayonnaise.

Your father came into the kitchen wearing what we call Gray
Mouse: soft sweatpants and a sweatshirt the color of light ash.
(There is also Oatmeal Man, when he wears his beige thermal underwear. You should know your father's other names, as I do.) Just
as the banana-split-making apparatus was in full swing, he said
to me, "Don't make me one."

I said, "Oh, I'm definitely making you one."

"All right," he said immediately, and went downstairs to go on-line. I brought him his split down there.

Hamburgers have also assumed a major role in my life. I have become ruthlessly carnivorous. I need big well-done ones in the middle of the day, sometimes two or three days in a row. French fries are not always necessary and yet sometimes rear their head; I eat them solely for the ketchup. I do not, however, want any of the ketchup to touch the hamburger. Well done, no red showing in the meat, and no condiments. I have given up on pickle slices and raw onions ever since I found out that they are vile mouth-ruiners and day-wreckers. I have been so blind.

We love the name Pablo for you. It feels warm and fitting. Also, what with Picasso and Neruda, it's fairly bullet-proof. We'll have to stock up on tiny berets and striped boat-necked shirts. It feels good to decide on a name early. Of course, I am unsure if it is us deciding or you.

You probably control names, too. Names and sun and food and beverage. And sleep. Oh, your arm has grown long.

I'm suddenly definite about keeping my last name in the mix. It just feels wrong to throw it away in the interest of economy or patriarchal tradition. Your father naturally wants to keep his name also. You may be saddled with a hyphen, but honestly, Pablo wouldn't have worked with just plain Friedman, so maybe you know what you're doing after all and wanted all three names.

It occurs to me now, at this moment, that the hyphen is another example of social tyranny. You are Pablo Finnamore Friedman unless you hear otherwise. No hyphen.

Meat meat meat meat meat meat meat meat.

I had to hit Burger King yesterday around three. I hadn't eaten since lunch. Then I drove home and threw away the bag so that your father wouldn't know. Did I also eat dinner? You know I did.

I've been battling insomnia on and off, have even resorted to sneaking half an Xanex now and again to tide me over. Fortitude to get me through the long Siberian pregnancy nights. The doctor's assistant looked Xanex up in the books and said it was okay but that she wouldn't do it all the time. Well of course she wouldn't, is what I thought. The monsters aren't chasing her at night, propping her eyelids open with anxiety sticks.

But finally my doctor told me about Benadryl. And baby, it is the pregnant woman's gateway to heaven. I had eleven hours of uninterrupted sleep last night, I mean I didn't even get up to pass water. That's how heavy it was. I'm going to Costco to buy it in the thousand-pill pak.

I will begin, almost idly, to think of a certain food, and by about the third or fourth day, it becomes an obsession, it becomes the only thing I can possibly eat next. It's like a toy bomb ticking, and the only way to dismantle the bomb is to eat clam chowder, the white kind. Or corn cakes with maple syrup and kiwi. I have also become deeply attached to long, thin baguettes toasted with butter and spread with honey. Let pie begin.

This is the time of real butter. It is the time of actual bacon and food without artificial sweeteners. I feel as though I have been let out of *jail.*

Today you are thirteen weeks old and already controversial. You should know that the mention of the name *Pablo* is alarming to a very few, highly insignificant people. From this palsied faction there is occasionally the slightest pause, and then, "Oh, really. Pablo." Then with a small, self-deprecating chuckle, they might tilt their heads playfully and say something like "Aren't you afraid people will think he's Mexican?"

Being Mexican is about the worst thing that these very few, highly insignificant people in Marin County can imagine. They habitually refer to them in a group, as *Mexicans,* a lump of persons exactly alike and not worthy of actual individual titles, like *Potatoes,* or *Beans.* To these people it's invariably Sebastian or Miles or Brice or other bank-president and future-CEO names, each one more tight-assed than the last. If I think about it too long, it makes me want to carry corn tortillas to whip out and start chewing on should the need arise. I find it amusing when they balk at Pablo, as though we were naming you *Jesus H. Christ* and jamming nails into our hands. They seem to feel your name is up for general discussion, like naming a local bridge or a stray cat.

"Hmmm. Mr. Whiskers? I don't like Mr. Whiskers. I like the name Blackie."

"Aren't you afraid people will think he's black?"

This is primarily an aberration. The vast majority, the quality people, love Pablo.

You will be dark-haired and dark-eyed, since your father and I both are, and our fathers were also, and both our mothers.

Your father's side of the family is French and German. Your great-grandmother Estelle had a dressmaking business and drove a car. Estelle once fell out of a plane and survived. The first night

I ever spent with your father, I dreamed of Estelle and her black sewing machine, and she held gold coins out to me.

My mother's side of the family is Spanish. You may inherit my family's skin coloring, which is light brown and some would say café. Both your great-grandmother Frieda and your great-great grandmother Rafina were from northern Spain. Rafina smoked cigars, drank whiskey, and in 1996, at the age of 104, she moved on. Back to the place where you came from. I wish you could tell me what that place is like.

Maybe you will, if I pay close attention.

Diana was here for three days, and the best part was that it didn't once rain. We went into San Francisco and had massages and lunch at Café Tiramisu on Belden Court. Potato leek soup, salad with gorgonzola and pears, and then spinach and cheese ravioli.

We ate every two hours, like infants. Our day went something like this: toast and decaf lattes, then a big breakfast in town, then ice-cream cones, a restaurant lunch around one, then back home for cottage cheese and fruit. Then we sat around, bloated and self-satisfied in lawn chairs, idly ordering your father about like two Roald Dahl characters. Around four o'clock, dual naps and a large early steak dinner, then cheesecake, then more toast.

It was about eleven A.M. Saturday, and we were having peanut butter and marmalade on English muffins, reclining on the front porch, and out of nowhere I said, "This is just a snack."

"Oh, I *know*," Diana said, a very serious expression on her face, eyebrows up into her skull. Lunch would be forthcoming, in other words. It fucking well would be.

Then, over Phyllis Giant Burgers, she and I formed UMM, which stands for Unfit Mothers of the new Millennium. Our pre- and postnatal mottoes include *Epidurals Forever* and *Benign Neglect . . . It Works!*

Diana is really showing, her belly is ripe. They say women show a lot sooner with the second baby. While she was here, I did feel a certain smug satisfaction in being able to still wear my old clothes, a very false sense of being on the right side of the tracks. I saw her glide past me to the bathroom for the tenth time that day and I felt an odd detachment. It was like looking at extremely old people in the supermarket and thinking, I'll never be like that. It's So Sad, you think, wheeling your basket of groceries along, maybe even moving a bit faster just to prove to yourself you can.

Of course, in a few weeks I am going to look just like Diana, and probably not even that good; she can still pull off a certain elegance with earrings and antique barrettes that I have never personally mastered. You'll see when you meet her, she has a style. I am going to be as big as she is and then I am going to go beyond, and then how the gods will slap their thighs. We will hear them roaring from way off.

Simone, your Jewish grandmother on your father's side, an unusually exuberant eighty-year-old Parisian woman in impeccable dress and hair, keeps calling you Pancho.

Your father suspects what she is up to, and he tells her, "Look, it's either Pablo or Pincus. Which would you prefer?"

She chose Pablo.

~

Fourteen weeks.

My fingernails and hair are amazing. Straight, shiny, and strong. Conditioner has become unnecessary. When I grow tired of writing or television or reading books, I just watch my hair and nails lengthen and thicken. I observe the luxury happening.

Saw my Singaporean hairstylist today. He revealed to me that in his appointment book, he separates people into categories on the basis of hair quality and thickness. He described how, in doing so, he can calculate the time involved with each client.

"It's like clay," he says. His long, thin fingers cup imaginary clay on an imaginary potter's wheel. "You can mold the clay. But you need a big piece of clay to start anything good," he says, spinning the imaginary wheel. "No matter how small the sculpture, you still want to start with big clay.

"You," he says, grabbing a handful of my hair, "you're Big Clay." He explains, "BC, I write in my appointment book.

"Your husband, he doesn't have so much clay . . ." His long fingers falter in the air.

"Low Clay," he says.

"LC?" I ask, tentative.

"Exactly. I write LC. Then I know how to budget my time."

"That's mean," I say, laughing hard.

"Then there are those who are really struggling. No Clay," he pronounces, as though he is saying *dead on arrival*. His hands fall to his sides. "Practically no hair at all.

"Those guys, I just have to make conversation. It's like 'Hey!' and 'Yeah,' and for twenty minutes, I move the same three or four strands around, spritzing product. We talk about where their next vacation is going to be.

"No Clays take a lot of vacations," he says.

After my haircut, I check our answering machine. Simone called today to say "Don't get sloppy," and to ask if I had gained any weight yet. Simone was one of the last Parisian Jews to escape to America before World War II, and she still has a thick accent. Her message also included the hitherto unknown fact that she had gained only fifteen pounds with your father. Setting the bar.

For my birthday present, she's sending me a gift certificate to Pea in the Pod. I saw one of their ads in *The New York Times Magazine,* of a nineteen-year-old supermodel with kohled eyes and hollowed-out cheeks, stick arms, and a big belly that I'm quite sure was a pillow. The tagline was *Pregnancy Redefined.* I wonder how many fortyish pregnant women with puffy cheeks and big necks and fat arms are committing suicide over this photograph. I'm thinking class-action suit.

As for your wardrobe, I purchased the smartest little navy-and-white-striped top. When we all decided on Pablo, that really set the tone. I feel instinctively that you are going to wear hats well but not foolishly, and be somewhat devastating to men and women alike.

You will face a difficult choice between sculpting and writing but will somehow juggle both and, despite being deeply ethical and artistic to the point of genius, end up quite conventionally well off, with a Manhattan loft in SoHo and a wife who has immaculate legs and wears, on occasion, red shoes.

I was driving down the hill this morning, and suddenly I could sense you sending me vibrations. I assume it has to be you. Or else I've gone completely Californian and will at any moment begin to use crystal deodorant and wear tie-dye clothing slathered with patchouli oil.

I felt my life as a vial. Inside the vial was the power I have, quite a bit, actually. And maybe I was using a fraction of what was available. If only I could see clearly, you indicated. It was like the Bible saying, Drop the scales from thine eyes.

I knew it was true. I thought of the time wasted deadening my senses and being sorry for myself and letting people run over me with their hard shoes. The way I sought out the people with the longest spikes on their cleats because that was what I thought would be the most fun and perhaps even what I deserved. I cried, grieving for the time I'd lost believing I was not good enough, not thin enough; teeth not white enough, hair not straight enough, breasts not firm enough.

And as I did this, I felt surprise and relief, knowing you were in fact my guide, not the other way around.

Now that I know you're XY chromosome, there are so many things I need to tell you about women, some highly sensitive intelligence that you would not otherwise possess. As I write this, I wonder if I am crossing over to the other side in some unforgivable act of treason.

Where to start.

Women need to look in the rearview mirror from time to time, to see if they have lipstick on their teeth. When you are old enough to drive, whatever woman you are with will grab the rearview mirror and twist it around to face her and apply her lipstick, and you will not be able to see anything in back of you until it hits you. (The same applies to drag queens, if you turn out that way.)

If you have been dating a woman for less than a year and she leaves you, she will never tell you the real reason. She will invariably say that she's not ready for a committed relationship right now, or that she just needs some space, both of which are at best half-truths. This doesn't mean that you're not great. It just means she's not for you, and she realized it before you did.

Women know who they're going to be with, and for how long, approximately ten minutes into a conversation. I knew with your father that I would marry him if at all possible. But before him, there was a man who I knew was temporary. And when I left him, I said, "I'm not ready for a committed relationship right now."

Women are trained not to hurt people's feelings, and odds are that we will not be truthful and say we hate your friends or your nose bugs us or you're smothering us to death or we've found someone we like better. A woman will not say that the sound of you eating toast, for example, makes her want to end her life. In fact, she will insist that it's the other way around. She will tell you that she's confused, she will apologize and say that she's just all messed up right now. *It's not you. It's me.*

A couple more home truths, and then we're done.

It is not true that women are naturally monogamous, any more so than men. I would hate for you to learn this the hard way, so I hope you never have to. I would also be sad if you were to abuse yourself with the notion that somehow sex matters to women less than men, or that women are any more or less honorable than men.

It also sometimes happens that while she is single, a woman may favor one man and date a second man as "insurance," someone to be with in case her primary man falls through. This may occasionally involve sleeping with both men in a closer time frame than one might prefer.

The best way to avoid this (assuming you are the primary man) is to make your commitment in a timely fashion. Then the insurance man will be let go, but not before.

Finally, be advised that most women know if you are lying and will do absolutely horrible things to get back at you for ever doing so, things you would never dream up. Women are secretive and capable of much. Stay on their good side and they will walk through fire for you. Otherwise, run, my son. Run like the mistral wind.

I was driving in my convertible across the Golden Gate Bridge, thinking two things.

First of all, I was thinking, This is the last spring I will be able to do this. Because you are coming. No one can stop you.

And because you are coming, I am going to sell my convertible. You can't even put a baby seat in it; also, I imagine that around the ninth month, it will be a wee bit tight. We will become utility-vehicle people, driveway parkers. No more tiny black convertible tucked in the garage like a shoe. Taking the long view, this is doubtless for the best. My car has no roll bar and is basically made of Philadelphia cream cheese, so I have been lucky to survive these past five years with a head. But I will miss the smell of the redwood trees as I head up Madrone to our house. I will miss being able to watch hawks soar. Something else I should probably not do while driving, another reason to lose the cream-cheese car. But I am feeling an advance nostalgia for these days, the convertible days. Now that you're hurtling toward us in twenty-six weeks, I know they are finite.

They always were, Voice says.

I saw Dr. Lorraine Gray again today. She announced that coming up very soon is the maximum weight-gain period, within which pregnant women gain a pound to a pound and a half every week, no matter what they eat. As she says this, I feel myself growing excited. Visions of whole fried chickens and country fries and black-and-tan sundaes dance through my head.

She couldn't find your heartbeat for about a minute that seemed at least an hour. She was moving the Doppler device over my swollen belly and explaining something about the blood test I was about to take. I couldn't hear her, all I could hear was the rushing of my own blood vessels as I listened madly for your heartbeat. Finally, there it was: *BOOM BOOM BOOM BOOM BOOM,* like a very fast bass drum, and I started to hear her talking again. Breathing resumed and I knew you were fine, probably laughing up your sleeve.

The blood test this time was called alpha-fetoprotein, for neural defects. I thought that was all over with the CVS, but apparently there is this last flaming hoop to pass through. More possibility for deformities, more shadowy doubts and waiting. Seven to ten days.

Tonight I call Diana.

"It's lonely." I say. "You'd think it wouldn't be, because the baby's inside of you."

"No," she says, interrupting me, preempting any other illusions I may be harboring. "It is an alone experience. The only time I feel the presence of the baby is when I'm alone.

"It's not at all the way movies seem," she says. "The husband who gives a flying fuck."

"Yeah," I say. But secretly, I know that your father cares a lot. He does give a flying fuck. So does Miguel, Diana's husband. He just can't show it right now because he's not used to the idea yet, and so he's busy falling off a cliff. Men worry about the money, women worry about the baby and the marriage and then money.

We all have our own separate cliffs, except for Diana and me. We share ours, like Thelma and Louise.

Even though I'm four months pregnant, it hasn't sunk in yet that I am going to be your mother. This is something that must be infinitely more apparent to you right now than it is to me. You're inside me and feeding off my calcium deposits and getting your protein and your oxygen from me. But I am on the outside, a place I have occupied most of my life. I don't remember what it's like to be on the inside.

I think what I'm lonely for is you.

I was a quiet child, saying almost nothing until I was three years old. I observed and waited, perhaps for something that still has not happened. At night I used to creep into the long hallway of our San Francisco flat and sleep in front of the wall heater; I clearly recall the line of gas flame and the cakes of dust around the coils, the gentle roar that meant heat was coming, things were working. I would also sleep at the foot of my brother's bed, which he allowed with a grace that has characterized our relationship. He has put up with me. I have tried to do the same. We each have a small beige birthmark on our knee.

I hid a dime that I had stolen from my mother's purse between the piano keys; she found it and started calling me a Sneak Thief. I stole a box of red candy hearts from the five-and-dime on MacArthur Boulevard and got caught. I remember the feeling of an old woman's hand hooking out from nowhere and grabbing my arm with surprising strength, terror squeezing my heart like a fist. I have always gotten caught; I see this now as fortunate. If you get away with things overmuch, you become intoxicated with your own skill.

I remember little girls as frightening creatures, cruel and exacting. If you didn't belong to some group, you twisted in the wind. I don't know how little boys are, and I'm not telling you to belong to some group, I'm just saying it's easier. You can belong to a small group that you like, or secretly be alone. The decision is yours. When it's your turn to die, no one is going to step forward and say, "Take me instead."

I hung out with Vicki Whitman and her younger sister, Lynn; they lived in an apartment building with a name, which I found exciting. I don't remember, but it was probably the Bel Air. Vicki was stick-thin and could vomit at will, a platinum blonde with transparent skin. I kissed Wilson, an Asian boy, behind the fence. I felt something vague run up my legs, which I filed for later.

We were poor but I didn't know it, due to the coupon strategies of my mother and her knack for rearranging furniture while we slept. I remember one day getting a new dress and how that felt, a terrible excitement welling in my chest. I remember the crisp feel of the cotton and the tag that was still on it, like a sign of royalty. I buy too many clothes now to make up for the fact that I had so few growing up. Of course, one can never make up. The best thing is to accept the vacancy and honor it, make it somehow part of you, not try to pretend it isn't there, or that you can compensate.

I remember going to the beach one day with Candy Estelita's family, the insane giddiness of pulling my bathing suit out of my bottom drawer, thinking to myself, I'm going to the *beach*. I remember so few family outings that when one happened to me, I knew I had struck accidental gold. I went places with other people's families. My own family was disparate; my father, I think, was practicing being divorced before the fact. My mother was working, though she stayed home until I was in kindergarten. That is a good thing, as it turned out, probably the only reason I didn't become a sociopath.

My father used to take me to the bathroom in the middle of the night when I was two or three years old. He would stand in the doorway and wait, then he would take my hand and walk me back to my bed. It is the best memory I have of him.

I can't remember the entire year my father, your grandfather, left home and divorced my mother. Out of all the things he took, this was the worst: my memory of being seven years old. I don't think we can forgive our parents their digressions, because we are unable to see them as people. They are our creators, which disqualifies them as people. To me they seem very much like inept and well-intentioned mad scientists.

Your grandfather has been dead now for twenty years and I have not forgiven him. If I am honest with myself, I have made a rock garden of his shortcomings, a labyrinth to meditate by, taking small steps always in a circle, leading back to where I began. I am not proud of this, nor is it as serene as it sounds. If anything, I grow more ill at ease as the years unfold and I see the damage unfurling, how I am unable to really trust happiness. But if you met your grandfather, it would be wonderful. He would make you laugh, tell you a few Jesus jokes, imitate the president with stunning precision. Everyone liked him; he didn't have to be their father, they could *afford* to like him. He didn't telephone them drunk in the middle of the night, weeping, on an episodic basis. He didn't take a year of their life in his cheap red plaid suitcase. He didn't stomp their childhood flat.

In junior high school, I wore thick black eyeliner and tried to look tough. I reapplied makeup before gym class. I rolled up my gym shorts and wore nylons underneath, which was against the rules. Rules were lovely when broken. I began breaking rules like dried spaghetti, just for the satisfying snap. I made friends with Diana, who wore no eyeliner and whose father still lived at home. She seemed popular yet attainable, unlike the Montclair girls, who lived in large hill houses. Montclair girls would never befriend a non-Montclair girl. If you sat down next to them, they'd drift off, afraid you would leave a stain. Montclair girls did not have to work at after-school jobs, they owned skis and aluminum tennis rackets, not wood. They drove horses and cars and paid for their gas with brightly colored credit cards, they were like complete adults already. They called their mothers by their first names and wore new clothes from the most exclusive stores, which were run by other Montclairians. If they could have had their own planet, they would have.

Diana's family were not from Montclair but owned their own home, an impressive and fascinating fact. In that home was Mr. Milosovich. I used to see him in the leather easy chair in the living room, he was *in there*, not divorced, not remarried, not wearing a Nehru jacket or knocking back screwdrivers in a fern bar; he drove a sensible American car and was still married to Mrs. Milosovich. No one was still married then, it was the seventies. Spouses were leaving home via a courtesy bus that circled the neighborhood every twenty minutes for Las Vegas, a logo on its side of a broken heart and a bag of money with wings. The license plate read TRYAGAIN.

Diana had a tiny waist and long straight hair and a concave stomach, which in the summer was consistently the color of Hershey's milk chocolate. I thought Diana was the most beautiful person ever. If I was ever going to be lesbian, it would have happened then, but it didn't. I liked boys. Boys liked me also, though not as much as they liked Diana. The right kind of boys liked Diana. The bad boys liked me. Maybe the black eyeliner had something to do with that. You attract what you project.

High school was painful in many ways, yet I liked seeing my friends every day without having to make plans. I so wanted to be like the popular Montclair girls with their new Cabriolets and navy cashmere V-neck sweaters and almost nonexistent breasts. They were sleek and refined as granulated sugar. I was the sugarcane: rough, dark. I had no boyfriend in tenth grade, a position of deep shame and alarm. I was a virgin. Steve the quarterback took me out for one date and promptly went back to his girlfriend, Leslie, who was a song girl. That's a cheerleader. Don't get me started on cheerleaders, they are a breed unto themselves, beyond even the Montclair girls. I wanted to be a cheerleader but couldn't do a cartwheel, so I pretended I didn't want to be a cheerleader. Sometimes, when you pretend something, it turns out to be true.

Now I have dreams that I am back in high school. They are sweet dreams.

If you wait long enough, everything becomes nostalgia.

I'm waiting to feel you move. What is called the quickening is next. It sounds as if you are this very rich and complicated pudding being made to thicken, to jiggle when poked with a spoon. It sounds like you are just about done. All the hands, feet, organs, eyes, nose, ears, fingernails in place. The creamy bones waiting to fan out, to begin leaving.

When people ask how I am, I say, "I'm waiting for movement." I may have felt you already and didn't know it. I'm feeling ignorant on all issues right now. I don't know how well I am going to perform as a parent. My own childhood was strange, irregular. I am going to have to go out and find a model somewhere in the next few months. A model of how it should be, how to do it right.

Woke up last night with a pain in my side. Hobbled to the bathroom, hobbled back. Still there in the morning, so I called Dr. Gray's office.

Within ten minutes, her assistant called me back. I guess for the doctor herself to call you back, you'd have to be expelling a kidney or something. There would have to be blood spurting out of your eyeballs.

Her assistant pronounced it ligament pain from the uterus. One side of a pregnant woman's body grows at a different rate than the other side to accommodate you. The side that grows slower is the side that gets to feel like it has been hit with a crowbar.

She asked me if it was on the right side. I said it was.

"Oh," she said. "Do you still have your appendix?" She tried to sound bright and unconcerned.

"Yes," I said, "why?" In the moment, I knew why. I felt a deep sense of foreboding, and something else—ignorance. I have done something wrong by still having it. I should have rid myself of all extraneous organs before even thinking about having you.

Turned out that since the pain was on my right side, there was a very slim chance it could be appendicitis and not just ligament pain. So, as the assistant said, we're going to be watching for that. Any nausea or fever or bleeding, I am to contact them.

"But this is normal, right?" I said.

"Oh yes," she said.

Okay. So long as it's normal.

Sweet Jesus.

I'm writing this while I am on hold with Apple. I bought a computer from them, and it has broken six times in the last eleven

months. Some tinkly New Age piano music is playing, and I am
being passed from department to department. You can expect to
spend at least an hour on the phone if you want to get anything
done. Businesses are hoping the consumer will eventually get tired
and hang up. I want to hang up now, but I won't because that
will mean they win, and I want to win. Just once I want to win.
I am going to try to beg them to send me a computer that works,
even though that is against the rules.

Now the music has changed, and it's an upbeat version of the
same New Age piano music, with high-pitched fusion synthesiz-
ers. It's the kind of music that makes you think of someone who is
in touch with their inner light but perhaps owns a gun. After
twenty-two minutes, someone answers, a woman named Christine.

"Thank you for calling Apple. May I have your name and telephone number, in case we get disconnected?"

I can't say this inspires huge trust. If they can't work a simple
telephone, how can they make laptop computers?

"What seems to be the problem?" Christine says.

"It's a lemon," I say. "You've replaced the motherboard twice,
the sound card twice, and both of the lithium batteries. I really
don't want to go into all that technical stuff all over again. Can I
just have a computer that works?" Honesty is best, baby. If nothing else, it saves time.

"Would you mind if I put you on hold while I check some resources really quickly?" she says, her voice suddenly tired. It is
almost five o'clock, and she sounds like she is not going to check
her resources, she is going to smoke a bowl of crack.

Back to the frenzied New Age piano. Now I am feeling torn; I
don't really want to send in my computer. It's broken and it's ridiculous, but I've gotten used to having it around. I must, must
not give in to the demons of technology. I must accept a huge
inconvenience in exchange for the promise of lesser inconvenience,
and a possible free upgrade.

She comes back on the line, sounding refreshed. "We are going to escalate your case to a senior agent. A senior agent is going to be able to discuss your options with you a whole lot better than I can.

"We're going to escalate this," she repeats, letting me know that this is a very big deal. Not everyone gets escalated. I am special. I have a special broken computer.

"Now I am going to give you your case number," she says. "Do you have a pencil?"

"Don't worry," I say. "I'm writing down everything you say on my computer. What did you say your name was?"

There is just the tiniest silence. "Christine." They never give their last names, baby. They don't want anyone to know who they really are. They don't want anyone showing up at their house with a funky laptop and a rope.

"Someone will be in touch with you by tomorrow, eight P.M. central time," she says. "A senior adviser."

"Okay," I say, defeated. "Thanks a lot."

"Thank *you*," she says. I can hear the relief flooding her voice as she realizes that she never, ever has to speak with me again.

The next day I beg and plead and come close to sobbing on the phone to the senior adviser, and I get my new computer and an upgrade. It is fine to debase yourself once in a while; the trick is knowing when, and of course when to stop.

Control, control, control. You have it, other people want it. That's it.

The ligament pain has subsided. I feel very happy, but I call the agency and tell them it's gotten worse.

Three-day weekend, baby!

I talk to your aunt Diana, and she is obsessing about her black socks, which she has lost. I understand this, having spent four hours last Sunday looking for a pencil sketch of your grandfather Richard that my first boyfriend, the artist, did in college. I couldn't relax until I had found it, which I did eventually, tucked inside his old journal which I'd salvaged from his flat.

Diana is leaving for New York tomorrow, on a field trip with six of her high school students from Portland.

"I'd really like to enjoy this trip," she says, only half joking. "But I can't find the black socks."

"Perhaps there will be other black socks in New York," I say.

"Yes, but those won't be the socks I had. They will be socks I bought in New York," she says. She sighs heavily. "I look like I'm ready to deliver."

Diana is only five weeks ahead of me. Unlike me, she is clearly pregnant; I just look as though I have let myself go.

Then she says, "I had a dream about Jason Black last night, only I made him taller."

We ponder this. Jason was her almost boyfriend in tenth grade.

"Nobody likes me," she says. She throws it away, like saying, Your fly's open.

These subjects may seem unrelated to the untrained eye, but they are not. Now, more than ever, I understand your aunt Diana so completely that it is like talking to myself, only more expensive.

"I'll be gone for four days and who knows what will happen to me," she says.

"Nothing's going to happen to you," I say. Ever, I think to myself.

"I know," she says. "But it's a good distraction."

"Call me when you get back," I say.

"I love you," she says. She always says that before she hangs up. And I always say it back.

Your biological parents are only a base. The friends you make growing up become your extended family.

I broke down and mail-ordered some maternity clothes from New York, finally. I was on the cordless phone, joking about how my hips are getting bigger, along with my breasts and thighs and fingers and neck and face and even the backs of my knees. And the woman said, "Oh, don't worry! I've got two kids and I've never been in better shape and I'm *thirty*."

I felt even more depressed and was about to say, Well, I'm almost forty. But then I stopped myself. She's a mail-order person in New York. I never have to meet her. To her, I can be any age I want. That would, I guess, have to be twenty-one. But I left it open.

You'll love twenty-one.

I sometimes feel a sense of unease. For not being the perfect, young, spry mother, the unblemished canvas you deserve. I have been fired three times, have been to jail once in New Jersey for four hours, and have had twenty-two lovers. Also I have several gray hairs, which I secretly pluck from my temples while sitting in parked cars outside McDonald's. Maybe I should have had you when I was younger.

I should not be telling you any of this. I should be strong enough to keep it in. But I am not, or if I ever was, I am no longer. Pregnancy strips off the veneer, the protective casing. It husks the soul.

You are opening me. In the end, I will split open and you will emerge. I have heard tell that this is the way of birth.

Pregnancy, by the way, is something you want to plan. Not everyone enjoys a surprise party that goes on for eighteen years and involves diapers.

When I was twenty-one, I was invincible. I was in my second year at the University of California at Berkeley. I wore Chinese-style clothing without looking ridiculous. I had shoulder-length glossy hair and could wear a bikini without serious doubts. Men stared at me and honked their horns wherever I went. I had a long horizontal Matisse poster in my bedroom and no money and a green Audi 100LS sedan that never ran. I arranged pink gladioli in a vase and kept a clear mason jar filled with pink marshmallow cookies in the same room, to pick up the color. Strangers would remark on the beauty of my eyes. I believed in the essential goodness of people. I didn't know then that the media is hostile, and that all but two or three of my friends were passing through. I believed in the level playing field and the honor of love. Men came knocking on my door late at night and I let them in.

When I was twenty-one, I knew I would marry young and have three children and a tall, elegant husband. I planned to learn French and Spanish and would skydive at some point, see the pyramids, own a horse.

I still believe many of these things.

I never thought anyone would be unfaithful to me or that serious unhappiness could touch me or that any of my friends would die. I spent huge blocks of time reading and writing poetry, I worshiped Anne Sexton and Richard Hugo and Mark Strand and Sylvia Plath and Adrienne Rich and Elizabeth Bishop and Walt Whitman and Wallace Stevens and Ezra Pound and the ubiquitous e. e. cummings. I inhaled the scent of literature and the discussion of literature, I laid my head down on wooden desks at Wheeler Hall and looked sideways out the tall windows.

I am starting to go back toward that place. I think you may have something to do with this. It is hard to be cynical when life is inside of you.

Lily Tomlin says that no matter how cynical you are, you can't keep up. And it is often tempting to be cynical. Just know that it is impossible to feel joy while you are feeling cynicism. It is like wearing tight shoes and trying to mambo.

Eighteen weeks as of yesterday. Felt a soft poke in my lower belly last night after eating an artichoke. Hard to tell what you were trying to say, or if it was you at all.

When I do feel distinct movement, I am going to document it exactly, so that people won't be confused as to what fetal movement is. All this *butterfly flutter* and *fish zigzag* stuff is absolute tripe. Nobody knows what butterflies feel like, they have no reference point for fish. These are both creatures that one rarely touches while they're alive, so what place do they have in an analogy for human sensation? None. I need accuracy and detail. I need crisp professionals; huge doses of truth and tactile exactitude.

Saturday night, my stomach looked at least six months pregnant. I was so bloated I could hardly move from room to room. As I walked, I groaned frequently, as a balm, a small audio comfort device. Your father then mentioned the word *hypochondria;* he used it in a sentence that applied to me. This just shows his ignorance, honey. He doesn't really know what's happening in there.

I think before a woman is really huge, before she looks like she is carrying a Louis XVI commode in her gut, people just don't take her aches and pains seriously. I can't help feeling a gun would help. Just a small pistol strapped to my side, and when I complained about feeling bloated or headachey or nauseated, I would lightly finger the pistol.

Last night I dreamed that I was trying to write my name, and I couldn't do it. I was with another woman, a famous writer, who said, "That's because you're changing so fast."

Later, as I drive into the city, I see the bay fog tumbling like clotted cream over the Marin Headlands, and I think, I should remember to tell you this. How swiftly it rolls, running for its life, the sun pushing from behind. It makes me think of labor, the time when you come. You will see for yourself when you get here. The fog, the hills, the bay, the sun. All of it.

I reflect on the fact that whatever happens, I will know there was once a time when you were inside of me. With my own mother, this fact has never seemed real or even particularly pleasant. I understand that it is something a mother experiences and not the child. You will forget where you were, this time of becoming. It will be a distant pull, a faraway sound, and then nothing.

I am here in these pages to remind you not of being inside me, but of what happened in the world before you could see yet still were.

I am your eyes.

Nineteen weeks. We're going in to see you tomorrow, on the sonogram; another depth dive. We're going to see detail today, which frightens and excites me. I feel like I am going to look closely at a confidential government file that is about me. I'm not sure what will be there, and there might be something I'm not prepared for. I'm wondering if they will count the extremities out loud.

I know one fact for certain: I will be the only tense person in the room. Maybe bursting into small fits of inappropriate laughter at any provocation. Simple phrases will confuse me, I'll need things repeated. The moment I don that blue backless gown and lie down on the examining table, I lose all my education.

I hope I won't embarrass you too much, but thankfully you can't see what's happening yet. I plan to dramatically clean up my act before you are able to see me.

There is also a part of me that is ecstatic. I'm going to see you, which is something I hardly ever get to do. I am going to see you. Will you wave or just be fetal? Your father says not to harbor expectations, you could be simply reclining. Thinking baby thoughts, of breasts and applesauce.

The truth about the pregnancy is, and I think I can be frank with you, that sometimes I just want it to be over and for you to arrive via FedEx. I like and even love parts of it, but they seem to just go on and on, like Robert Duvall in *The Apostle.* Sometimes I feel like a joke, a burgeoning breeder, a test dummy. *Let's see what happens if we blow her up. Okay, now twist her intestines into a knot. Now spin her around real fast, so she loses her center of gravity.*

And the worst part is, it's only just begun. They are devising even more horrible tests every second, baby. And the final test will involve pain, I know it. There is going to be *pain.*

I would do this only for you.

That's a lie. I am doing this for myself. Like I said in the very beginning: *selfish.*

The second sonogram. The white-coated technician woman puts the lotion on my belly and attaches the Doppler portable-razor thing, and there you are. You are on your stomach, balled up tight inside of me, and won't turn over, a curved white shape with a skull and what looks like four legs but is actually two arms and two legs. Thank goodness.

They check your heart, which is beating in that disco-inferno strobe-light way of yours. They count the chambers of your heart; you have the requisite four.

They slowly scan your brain from the top, and the technician says, "He's got a wonderful brain."

I remember she said *wonderful*. I mark that for later, something to dwell on for a long time. Waves of pleasure and pride furl over my body. Mensa, here we come. I will retire young, very young.

We begin to run short on time, and you still haven't turned over for your profile shot. They leave me and your father alone for a few minutes to wait for the head doctor. I climb down off the table and jump around, shouting, "Turn over! Turn over!"

The doctor comes in, shoots one last picture. In this one, we finally see your face. You have drifted onto your back at the last moment. Then you flip back, hiding once again. Like a movie star, you give us a glimpse but no more. *No pictures today, please. But thank you for your interest.*

At home we examine the last sonogram shot.

This cannot be right. Although slightly blurry, you are serene and mature in profile. You look like a tiny captain of industry.

If you keep the tags on everything you buy, you can return it months later, after you've had the whole retail experience and the pleasure of owning it and maybe even wearing it once.

I returned a DKNY jacket today at Saks because I am not going to be able to wear it again until you're about two. The sales clerk gave me a lot of grief about crediting it back to my American Express card because part of it was purchased on a gift certificate, and he had to call for a manager and then he ran out of cash-register tape, and after about fifteen minutes he rubbed his forehead and said, "I really hate this. I could get into a lot of trouble for doing this incorrectly. . . ."

"Yes, but I don't care," I immediately said. The words just flew out of my mouth like birds.

Something about having you inside of me releases truth serum into my bloodstream. I may have to give up circulating in the world if it gets any worse.

Today I am experiencing life as richly as a child again. I'm not sure how this has happened.

Madonna, who secretly is my hero and who has a new CD out, says that when she gave birth to Lourdes, she was reborn. For me it's already happening. I believe it has to do with purifying oneself; everything one has to give up to be pregnant. Giving yourself over to the unknown, and another feeling without a name. Language would betray it.

You can hear now. Your inner ear has formed.

I shout *"I love you"* into the bedroom. Then I feel stupid. Then I don't. This is pretty much the story of my life.

Your father is at a client dinner, and I am at home watching television. Since our local cable system upgraded, we now have eighty channels. I move like a crocodile through them, spooning cereal into my mouth. In my twenty-first week, I have settled exclusively on Wheat Chex.

I pause on a channel where a large woman with heavy eye makeup is belly dancing in a brightly lit studio. At first I think she is pregnant—probably why I paused here—but upon second glance, I see that her face is too old, just. Wearing a black leotard and red harem pants with sequins on the hips, she is dancing confidently on a white and black faux leopard rug and chanting, "Snake arms . . . rib cage . . ."

I watch as she balances a sword on her head and undulates. I am transfixed among several emotions. She then switches her position, bringing the sword in her right hand repeatedly up to her forehead and away, saying into the camera, "You're letting a story be told . . . leaving some things up to the audience's imagination."

The music shifts and she goes offstage to get something, then she comes back right away, holding out two small glass jars. "All right, that's just some little fun we can have with a sword . . . next let's try hand candles."

When she swings her hips toward the camera, balancing the sword on her head and the lit candles in her hands, I start to be genuinely impressed.

"Make a ceremony out of it," she says. I lift the spoon to my mouth.

Your movements are pronounced now. It feels like the world's smallest kickboxer with cotton wrapped around his tiny feet and everything encased in flat champagne. That's how it feels.

Someone blowing soap bubbles behind my navel.

Angel gas.

~

I am at the library getting out a guidebook on Italy for our upcoming trip, and everyone is dead quiet. This is the way libraries always are, baby. Libraries and white-people churches.

Then the librarians start talking to each other, their voices quite natural, as if there is no one else in the room. There are two of them, one of whom looks exactly like a librarian and the other who resembles a professional weaver or a maker of organic cheese, which is not so far off from looking like a librarian, if you live in Marin County.

"Thanks for cleaning that book . . . I had been meaning to get to it. It was just filthy, there was some sort of crusty material on it. . . ."

There is a small, different silence as everyone in the library pretends not to be listening. I am probably the only one who finds this remark hilarious, but I act as impassive as the rest, who are thumbing through magazines in the wingback chairs, exactly like extras on a set of people at a small-town library. At this point the telephone rings, a person calling to renew books. A moment or so after hanging up the receiver, the cheese maker says to the other one, "Yes. She's been pretty sick, you know."

They appear to know exactly who they are referring to. I'm betting it's the book-renewal woman, who I intuit is around a hundred by the loud, excessively polite voice that was used during her phone call, which now, unbeknownst to her, has played its part in a kind of afternoon radio show for the rest of us.

"She's going into the hospital Monday. It's pretty serious."

"Really?"

"Oh yes. They have to do a colostomy."

Then, unbelievably, the cheese maker says, "How do they do that?"

"Well, you know, I *asked* her. Because I've always been fascinated with that . . ."

And as I look around the bookshelves, everyone is still looking exactly as before. Their faces are stone, they are the perfect People at Library, nothing is going to shake that, no matter what the librarians say or do. This, I am thinking, is what becomes of children.

I am oddly surprised when people know I am pregnant just by looking at me. I prefer the earlier phase, when strangers didn't know unless I revealed it to them, like a card trick.

Right now I am still at the stage where, depending on the cut of my clothes and the abuse of the color black, how far along I appear is variable. In the same day, one woman remarked that I didn't look five months pregnant *at all,* and another person—a man—upon hearing I was five months along, said, "Hmm. You're big."

It goes without saying whom I intensely disliked after which remark.

Sometimes I catch an unguarded glimpse of myself in the mirror, chesty, hips wide, and no apparent neck, and I feel terrible. Being thin is what people expect you to be if you're a woman. I am pregnant, I am nowhere near thin. I am on a whole other continent.

Yesterday I came across something that Walt Whitman wrote.

Be not ashamed women, . . .
You are the gates of the body, and you are the gates of the soul.

I'm driving to work, and I'm playing "Mezzanine" by Massive Attack, and suddenly I feel you moving with an odd insistence.

I am almost sure you are dancing.

Thursday, a gorgeous day. I cross the Golden Gate Bridge with the top down. I feel I look glamorous: dark glasses, hair pulled back, black filmy scarf, and since I'm sitting down in my car, people can't tell I'm pregnant. This fact seems enormously important; I file it away.

To my right there is a yellow bus with the words UPPER LAKE UNION SCHOOL, and I think there must be a few envious high school students looking down at me in my shiny clean black convertible and my adulthood, and I slide my eyes sideways to check. And all I see is the backs of dresses and pants because they're all standing up, looking in the opposite direction, toward the view.

They pull ahead of me and I notice that the back of the bus says STOP WHEN RED LIGHTS FLASH, which, when you think about it, is premium advice.

We leave for Italy tomorrow.

Twenty-four weeks. We arrive at the seaside hotel in Viareggio. Our room has not one but two balconies, a magnificent view of the Riviera, thin slivers of soap. There is a breakfast menu on the back of the door, coffee and rolls sent on a tray to our bed for a somewhat indecent fee, if we want them. We always do. No free shampoo, no shower caps. They're having none of that. Nothing worth stealing from European hotels. In American hotels, it's fine to take the little bottles of shampoo and bath gel, but not the robes. In Europe, you bring your own robes almost all the time. They're not taking any chances over here: We're Italy. We don't need robes.

Your father removes his watch for a nap. There is a white space on his wrist where the watch was today as we lay on the sunny beach. It seems like a secret place, a place that only I will ever know about. You have a secret place also, where you are.

He puts on an eye mask, and he says, "What's weird is knowing there's light out there, but you can't see it."

With his black eye mask and swarthy skin, your father looks alarmingly like Zorro.

I stay up and read about Venice, our next stop. It seems impossible, a city built on water, suspended on what seems like sheer lunatic belief. But it must be possible. We are going there.

We entered Venice in a motorboat that banked directly to our hotel pier, close to the Bridge San Michel. It was stunningly romantic.

Your father felt you move for the first time the next morning. We were just about to get up and go sight-seeing. I placed his hand on my stomach and, when you gave a good hard move, I said, "Did you feel that?"

"Yes," he said. Then he kept his hand there, and every time you moved, he said, "Hmm" in this very pleased and sleepy tone, and I laughed every time.

The date is May 21, 1998.

At a sports bar in Venice, we are watching the gondolas glide by like money-sucking black eels. Your father is wearing his favorite khakis and a black T-shirt, I am wearing maternity clothes with horizontal stripes.

"Is there anything about pregnancy you didn't expect?" he asks me.

"Everything," I say without hesitation. As I say this, a wraith-like Italian girl sips a frappé rum drink nearby. I resent her deeply. I resent her whole freewheeling nonpregnant persona.

The fact is that I never thought about the pregnancy at all. I didn't consider it.

In the Saturday-morning cartoons I watched as a child, the lazy-eyed stork brings the baby, sometimes to the wrong house. He is usually wearing a deliveryman's cap. The stork flies casually on large white loping wings and drops a diapered newborn down the chimney. This is the same chimney Santa Claus shimmies down with his sack of goodies. You were conceived around Christmas. This is lodged in my subconscious along with the stork cartoons. Together they form a union of ignorance.

If I had thought about the nine months of pregnancy in any meaningful way, perhaps things would be different now, but I doubt it. Because I always believe I can beat the odds: the normal rules of life don't apply to me. Massive evidence to the contrary has no effect on this belief, which renews itself like skin cells.

It's our last morning in Italy. Sun filters through the red wooden window shades, the sounds of boats on the canal swell. Before I am fully awake, I hear your father say from just behind my left ear, "Will you marry me?"

"Yes," I answer, not turning around. The fact that we are already married seems to make this proposal gossamer, not to be disturbed.

"Okay," he says, "we'll set a date sometime before the baby gets here."

I think he has gone back to sleep when he says, "I'll never let anything bad happen to you."

~

First day back at work after the vacation. My voice mail contains a cheerful account executive dictating the small copy for a print ad at 11:54 P.M. last Wednesday. Apparently no one told her I was in Italy, or else the excitement of the project overwhelmed her and she disregarded the physical distance in favor of an immediate communication.

"Instead of saying 'Causes burning,' let's say 'May cause mild burning' . . . or, I know!—'Some women have experienced mild burning, but the sensation was usually temporary.'"

It takes twelve hours to get to Italy, but it takes only one voice mail like this to return from Italy.

I revise about a hundred ads, or what seem like a hundred ads and are only five. I go to lunch with my partner, Gavin, to Nan King. We stand in line and are ritually abused by the owner's wife, who comes out periodically with a broom to manicure the long line. There are too many people who know about the food, the best Chinese in the city. We are here for the Nan King chicken, which is sautéed with oyster sauce and sweet potatoes and snow peas. It is the Nan King Chicken of Death, so sublime we almost don't mind the woman with the flailing broom and the look of accusation. She is the test all must pass to obtain the prize. Also, she drives some tourists away who don't understand her.

Once inside, the restaurant is nothing but an alley halved by a grill with bar stools; additionally, maybe ten or twenty tables the size of place mats and chairs are jammed together into near-spatial impossibility. This, too, is part of the challenge. The owner's wife patrols the restaurant; one must shout out drink orders to her. She may hear you or not, depending on her mood and the status of the line outside. The owner himself will take your food order and then violently disagree with whatever you want. He is not predictable and can force you into squid if crossed. We have found it is best to order the Nan King chicken every time, along with the onion cakes. Those items are fail-safe and meet with grudging approval and a slapped-down receipt, added up in Chinese and presented before the food has arrived.

We walk back to the office, stopping at the City Lights bookstore, where Gavin can buy art books from which to glean visuals and/or styling examples for our next project: a nefarious new business assignment that somehow, in some way, involves cats. This is all we have been told thus far. Gavin buys only six books, a slim load for him. He has recently been warned against the overzealous nature of his concepting expenditures. This happened because he went over the line. Gavin spent $700 on circus music, which flagged the system. A worried man with a red tie keeps poking his head into our office to ask about the circus music, whether he can see it or talk to Gavin about it. Gavin, of course, refuses. Gavin is going to be a director someday very soon. He, too, is on a ship, but not the baby ship. At only twenty-eight, he is not headed that way yet. But we match each other in stride as we walk, happy. Full.

Today your father got up at eight A.M., which is late for him. He turned to me clutching his lower back and said, "The baby really takes it out of me." He's still getting sympathy symptoms. His feet were killing him in Europe, just like mine.

Then, when he got dressed, his pants were slightly too tight. He expressed concern and disgust at his recent weight gain, maybe three pounds. "Yes," I said, "but you still have a *waist.*"

I feel this is like Gloria Vanderbilt complaining that she can't buy Paraguay.

Do not attempt to win approval from people in high places, especially those with impressive titles that include the words *New York* or *National*. These people run things, mostly, which is what makes this advice so difficult to follow.

In matters of work, it is also a grave error to try and please everyone. In general, the populace will be divided into four groups: 1) people who understand and appreciate what you are trying to do; 2) people who understand what you are trying to do and don't appreciate it; 3) people who don't understand what you are trying to do but appreciate it anyway; 4) people who don't understand what you are trying to do and hate your guts.

It is not important that everyone fall under the first category, it is only important that everyone participate.

There will be critics in abundance, critics are hiding behind bushes and inside armoires and underneath lawn chairs. Anyone can be a critic; it is the only job that has no prerequisites. But not everyone can play the flügelhorn. Remember that.

I've always been shortsighted. For example, you could say that mosquitoes keep Earth from hurling off into a meteor field and instantly exploding into a fiery ball, and I would say, "Yesss, but I sure do hate mosquitoes."

So even though I wanted you desperately, there is a part of me that doesn't understand why I'm getting so melon-y, so big. So pregnant-looking. Just in the last three days, I've nearly doubled. I don't know what to add to that. I hope to have some marked emotional growth and a surge of maturity and depth soon.

The thing is, I don't want to give anything up. I don't want to trade one for the other, like my figure, or the relationship I enjoy with your father, for you. I need to extract some kind of verbal agreement from your father, and I go into the living room and I tell him what I need from him, I tell him I am not willing to trade. And he promises I won't have to, that we will still love each other and be happy, that I will get my figure back.

But of course these are only words.

～

I talk to Diana, and she explains that she really and truly does not want to have a C-section this time. She says that what with the drugs and the numbness, you don't even feel like you've given birth. And that frequently, as in her case with Carmen, the doctors decide to do the C-section only after thirty-two excruciating hours of labor.

I tell her how delivery doesn't seem real to me yet, and that I have only recently accepted the conceptual accuracy of it, even though I am six months pregnant and look like I'm wearing a catcher's vest from the inside. I know intellectually that I'm going to have a baby, and I suppose that means delivery, although in a small corner of my mind I can't picture it and it's not a sure thing yet.

"It's like Africa," I tell her. "It's faraway and strange and you know it's there, but you've never seen it."

"Well, girl, you're gonna see Africa," Diana says. "Believe me."
I do. Her I believe.

The UPS man drives up to our house just as I'm watering the marigolds. As he hands me two packages, both of which contain baby books, he says, "How long?"

He can be talking only about one thing, I realize. I am down to one thing.

"September," I say.

He grimaces. Says there are three or four other women on this route who are also due. "The baseballs are wiven pretty tight this year," he says, shaking his head and smiling.

I've made a decision to begin lying about when I'm due and tell people August instead of September. The UPS man looked almost sorry for me, and I just can't take that kind of pity from strangers who hear the word *September* and whose faces telegraph, You mean you have to walk around like that for three more months? Jesus.

Not only am I going to start lying and saying August instead of September, I tell Diana that she should lie and say July, since she's due in August. She agrees.

"I can't believe I didn't think of it first," she says.

I heard the evil siren song of Baby Gap today and I went inside, helpless and a little disgusted. My heart beat faster as I saw the rows and rows of perfect minuscule clothes, clothes I or your father would like to have if they came in our size.

There was a floor display that said NEWBORN, and on it were these tiny French-blue viscose twin sets with mother-of-pearl buttons for $95. You would outgrow it while I'm buttoning it up, but you wouldhave had the status of receiving something that nice at some point in your life.

Ninety-five dollars, I thought. Why not just throw bags of money out of a helicopter?

Then I bought a black diaper bag for myself and a red-and-white-striped onesie for you that was on sale, and a yellow one that wasn't, with a monkey on it. And two finger puppets, an elephant and a dog.

~

Your grandmother? Her mother, your biological great-grand-mother, gave her up at birth.

Her name was Isabelle Garcia, and she was born in Lajas, Puerto Rico, and she conceived a child with Saul Mendez, who was born in northern Spain. Soon afterward Saul came to New York and married another woman. He had plans. This new baby, my mother, was not part of them. Yet my mother was raised by Saul's sister and mother, also from Spain.

There is a picture of my mother, age two, standing on the boat docking in New York. Isabelle stayed behind. No one knows why, except that she had to. My mother's adoption number is A-947, New York City. Her adopted name is Iris; they named her Iris because that was the name of the saint on the calendar on the day she was born: May 12, 1935. Her time of birth is unknown, as she was a home delivery in Mayaquez. Isabelle signed the birth certificate.

Isabelle is rumored to be dead, alive, a witch, a *bruja*. It is all very black.

My mother's only recollection of Isabelle is this. when she was still a small child, she was summoned to an apartment. Isabelle was sitting in a chair in the dining room with a man by her side. She was wearing a simple black dress, and my mother noted with wonder how their faces looked alike, hers and Isabelle's. The woman wore a little gold cross around her neck and her hair was curly. She could not speak English and was crying. The man (who was her lawyer) said she had come from Puerto Rico to ask if my mother wanted to go back with her. My mother did not. They took her downstairs—never said a word—and put my mother in a taxi back home. She was excited, as she had never been in a taxi.

When my mother got home to 1568 Second Avenue, she ran upstairs to tell her mother of this adventure. Frieda was alone in the kitchen, sitting at the table and crying. She was crying so hard that my mother started to cry.

After that, my mother was curious about Isabelle but it was a forbidden subject. Years later she found letters written in Spanish —her mother Frieda had hidden them—and read them all and put them back. To this day she can't talk about Isabelle to the family; they get upset and will not talk about her.

How could Frieda hide those letters? I don't know. This is all so tiring.

Saul did not acknowledge my mother as his daughter until he was dying. He died within weeks of Isabelle. Maybe she had something to do with that, had taken back some power and made it into a fist.

Maybe she isn't dead at all. I have learned to believe nothing.

There is a mystery surrounding this woman that will never be solved. I know that now. No one who would actually know anything can be trusted to tell the truth, it is so deeply buried, and no one really wants to know. Strange, isn't it. We have let part of our own family die: her punishment for giving up my mother, for not being right somehow. Part of our tree was broken a long time ago. I am sorry for Isabelle and for my mother and for my-self and for you, but there it is. Trees need tending, baby. They can die, a fact people are always surprised by.

My friend in Texas, Rob, is into cereal, although he is not pregnant. He's just always had an affinity for cereal. I met Rob the same year I met Diana.

"So what do you have at home?" I ask him.

"We probably have eight or nine different ones," he says. "Ranging from Grape-Nuts and Product 19 to Wheat Chex to Alpha-Bits to Sugar Pops. And then we have the major standby, which is Frosted Flakes.

"The kids don't get to touch the Frosted Flakes," he says.

"My boys and I sit at the table and read the sports sections and eat two to three bowls of cereal apiece."

Rob's sons are nine and five years old. Rob says, "So what the five-year-old's been doing is, late at night he goes in my gym bag, into the toiletry bag, and takes the soap out of the plastic travel-soap container. So I get into the shower at the gym and I have no soap because he's got it. I mean, he just does crap like that all the time."

"What's that about?" I ask.

Rob says, "He's just fucking with me. 'Don't touch this stuff in here.' I told him specifically. I get up at like five-thirty A.M., so I pack the night before. He gets in after me, though.

"One time I get in there after my gym shower, and there's no underwear. Gone. He doesn't do it every night, because then I'd catch on. He thinks it's funny."

"It *is* funny," I say.

Rob says, "When your VCR gets stuffed full of foreign objects, you'll see how funny it is."

"What's he put in there?" I ask.

"Toys," he says with disgust. "Also, you know, I make tapes to work out with at the gym. The other night I've got the stereo on, and I'm making a new tape, and it doesn't sound right. So I walk over to the big column speakers. And from a certain angle, I see something weird in there, and so I take the Styrofoam front matting off.

"He had stuck his finger into the tweeters or woofers or whatever they are and put dimples in all of them. He did it to both of them. Then he put the black Styrofoam back on."

"That's funny, too," I say.

"I cannot fucking wait," he says, "until Pablo gets here."

Me either.

I tell Rob how I'm thinking of converting to Judaism, so that when you're born, you'll be something.

"Right now," I said, "he'd be squat."

"There's a lot to be said for squat," Rob says.

Have one friend in Texas. When you badly need to laugh, call your friend in Texas.

I must say the parent's literature is depressing. It describes how after the baby is born, marriages get strained and often fail, about how your life will never be quite the same ever again, and that it's still good just different, all very vague and disturbing. I cannot believe this is true, but then why do they write it in books? And if it is true, then why the unbelievable pressure to procreate in the first place? It's like a terrible trick played by society, especially everyone who already has children and all potential grandparents.

It is expected for women to breed, but the moment you do, they come at you with reams of information pronouncing doom, crippling stress, and general malaise. And what's maddening is how even though I'm almost forty years old, they all know so much better than I do. I'm the first-time pregnant village idiot.

If one more parent says, "Do it now. This will be the *LAST TIME EVER* you can _____," with that ominous, hypernegative tone, I am going to scream.

If I were you, baby, I would be very upset and up in arms. I would be picketing with little Popsicle-stick pickets.

MEDIA UNFAIR TO BABIES

PARENTS OUT OF U.S.

You move often now. It's kind of comforting. I know you're alive and active, possibly doing hand shadows against the wall of my uterus.

I should swallow some LEGOs, or a bat and ball.

Now, when people at the office say hi to me, their eyes immediately stray to my stomach. From my stomach their eyes drift off altogether, they don't ever come back to my face. It's like, Well, that's the end of that story.

I feel irrevocably ordinary. You're inside me and magical, but no one can see you yet. They just see this big brown woman headed like a ship toward them with big arms and a big neck and eyes that say, Help me.

They just see Big.

It's odd that we forget being born, forget the biggest thing that ever happens to us. It's easy to see how one would want to forget having your head and body pushed through a vagina. Going from a place that is totally safe and warm to one that is not guaranteed to be either.

We of course will do our best.

Frank Sinatra died today.

Famous people go in threes, baby. So it was Frank Sinatra, Phil Hartman, and Barry Goldwater.

"The triumvirate is complete," your father said. "It will be safe for a while now."

Sinatra was the greatest singer of our century. He was also an actor, won Oscars and Grammys and practically every honor that exists. I'll play you some Sinatra this afternoon when we lie down for our after-work nap. "Witchcraft" was my favorite song of his.

His last words were "I'm losing."

In other headlines, 169 FEARED DEAD ON KENYA AIRWAYS FLIGHT. The plane crashed into the ocean at a thousand miles per hour, burst into flames, and a day went by. The media should face up to the fact that things have indeed come to a head. It should say 169 DEAD PEOPLE WE HAVEN'T FOUND YET.

This morning Gavin and I attend an agency-wide meeting where we are told not to worry and how great everything is going, even though 10 percent of the staff are at that moment being led into a big room and fired. The velvet glove of upper management has once more dispensed of a few random bodies.

Afterward, Gavin and I scurry back to our office. We have survived another bloodletting. We lock the door in case they try to come for us. We draw the shades and put our feet up. It is understood there will be no advertising created this day, in honor of those who have passed from us. Sitting in the semidark, we discuss the flawless technique of the corporation, their high marks in ruthlessness, dishonesty, and overall stupidity. After about an hour, we move on to other subjects.

Gavin tells me that even though I'm six months gone, I am not getting fat all over like some women do. "You're getting more pregnant, not more fat," he says.

Then he says that I actually look thinner than I did before in the face and neck.

If you look long enough, baby, there is always someone who will tell you exactly what you want to hear.

Your father's birthday is this next Sunday. He will be fifty, and he has been keeping careful track in the media of who else is fifty.

"There are two fifty-year-old men who I definitely want to look younger than when I'm fifty," he says, "Newt Gingrich and Rush Limbaugh.

"I'd also like to look younger than Warren Beatty when I'm fifty," he says, "but he's sixty-three."

Twenty-six weeks next Monday.

I went to Dr. Lorraine Gray, and her assistant weighed me and I made the error of looking down at the scale after I had stepped on it. A hundred and sixty-eight pounds.

"Let's just say one-seventy," she says.

I want to grab her by the throat, but I don't.

I'm beginning to accept the fact that you're coming in September. And I know that you are not a mistake, that you are meant for me. It was Miles Davis who said, "Don't worry about making mistakes. There are no mistakes."

This is all I have for you today.

As instructed, I drank the bright orange glucose drink this morning and they took some blood, two vials. I have given countless vials of blood to these people, they are insatiable vampires.

Now they are checking to see if I have pregnancy diabetes, but you and I know that's nonsense. It implies imperfection on one of our parts, a notion I am not in the mood to entertain today.

Mommy is having a good-hair day. Hair, for reasons unknown to us, is of vital importance here. I have no idea why.

Last Friday at the office, someone said my hair looked wonderful. And I have been clinging to that remark, sucking on it like a lozenge ever since. You'll understand when you get your real hair, not just the faux fur that's covering you right now.

The crib is up. It converts into a toddler bed and has five drawers.

Whenever I glance at it out of the corner of my eye, in what used to be your father's home office, I think to myself, "Why is there a crib in that room?"

~

I was driving through North Beach, and I passed a gaggle of Italian construction workers, one of whom said, "Can I go with you?" The others made whistling, keening sounds.

They didn't know about you, baby, or else maybe they would have been more respectful.

There are some of your gender who feel a need to cry out in the street to women. I used to feel they were wrong and inappropriate; now I am not so sure. Now I feel like flinging them signed blank checks.

~

Seven months.

I remember when I was newly pregnant with you and I ran into my friend Sam, whom I used to work with. I announced, before even saying hello, that I was pregnant. That was when this news could be brandished, like a weapon.

I told him and he said, "How far along?" and I said, "Eleven weeks." And he said, "Oh. You're still counting in weeks."

The best compliment I ever received was from Sam. We were in his office discussing something dry and businesslike when he looked up at me and paused, and said, with a straightforward expression, "Is this as beautiful as you get, or do you get even more beautiful?"

I will never forget that.

When you have become a man, I hope you will understand about compliments.

~

This morning I go out to get *The New York Times,* and there on the front porch is half a rat. The back half. Which leads me to think—where's the other half? And I want to think it's a mouse, but a quick glance at its size assures me that no, it's a rat.

I immediately call Mad Augusten.

"We're all only half a rat away." That's what Mad Augusten says the message is. We laugh maniacally.

Then we eat breakfast on the phone together. I have a bagel with low-fat Philadelphia cream cheese, he has a filet mignon and gorgonzola cheese sandwich from Dean & Deluca. This is the difference between California and New York.

~

I am officially in my third trimester. You've become more real to me, and to your father. For the first time since we found out I was pregnant, we speak of you as if you are really coming to live with us. Maybe.

To mark this passage, I bought some pacifiers yesterday, the kind that *The Girlfriends' Guide to Pregnancy* recommends: Mini Mam. They looked vaguely European, which was one of the other reasons I bought them. I also bought newborn drawstring nightgowns, two for $9.99. And two four-ounce bottles, and two sets of bottle nipples. I did not believe I should have been doing this, buying those baby things in that baby store, but as I made my way toward the checkout counter, no one said anything, so I guess I am not going to be confronted about it. Your father just followed me around the store, looking deeply uncomfortable. As though I were shoplifting.

Your great-grandmother Frieda called my mother last night crying because Aunt Juana had just died, quietly, in her sleep. She said that Juana had so many plans—she was an avid gardener. My mother asked her, "Mom, how old was Juana?"

Frieda answered, "Only a hundred and one."

All the women in my family live a long time. They just start to get good in their seventies and eighties. There's something to be said for plain endurance.

I dreamed that I was in a large white rectangular birthing room, watching two women in labor. They were both partially clothed and hanging suspended on metal racks, which was the normal procedure, it seemed to me, for labor.

One of the women in labor was doing quite well, efficiently popping out her baby as I watched. This woman then caught her baby, bounded around in a semicircle, and ran out of the room, head held high like Jackie Joyner-Kersee.

The other woman was screaming.

Twenty-nine weeks.

First thing in the morning, you begin jabbing the middle of my stomach and somersaulting. Then you do something that feels very much like a slow fox-trot. You seem extremely active, on a progressive level. To tell the truth, and I don't mean to sound judgmental, I honestly don't understand what you're *doing* in there.

Your father says, "Practicing."

I put your clothes in the appointed small crib drawers. It seems like a tremendous act of faith.

After you are here, I will try not to become one of those parents who brag incessantly about their children, who force them to recite the alphabet backward or sing the Lord's Prayer in German to horrified dinner guests. One of those parents who tell people who aren't interested and haven't asked what their progeny's grade-point average is, what school they go to, how handsome and brilliant and psychic they are.

If something goes awry and I do become one of those parents, you have my permission to sneak into my bedroom while I am sleeping and pinch my nostrils shut.

After your father made me lasagna, I was lying down, and you went into a very aggressive rolling action that sent the skin on my stomach undulating. Your father calls you the Rumba Champion of Larkspur. Tonight he leaned down into my stomach as if it were a microphone, and he said in this very conspiratorial tone of voice, "As soon as you're born, bond with *me*."

The lasagna was superb, by the way. People love to be cooked for. I snagged your father with soup.

If there is someone you love particularly well, make her something good to eat. Then wait. She may very well wander back to you for more, like a cat.

~

Saw Dr. Gray yesterday. She had the Doppler gadget on my belly, listening to your heartbeat, and you kicked right into it. BOOM. Back off, Mama.

She seemed startled. I like the fact that you can already startle doctors.

I asked her if she thought it would be all right if I worked right up until delivery, and she said no. I told her I still feel good, which I do. And she said with perfect assurance that the last month will suck the life out of me. Or medical terms to that effect.

"But Doctor, you don't understand," I said. "I am not like ordinary folk. I have the power to override the bodily functions that drag down others. I can just decide to be normal and energetic, and I will be.

"Plus, I may not even have this baby in September. If I decide to, I can postpone it indefinitely."

None of this really happened, except in the recesses of my mind. Which is still in denial not of you, but of the whole insane physical, mental and medical process.

I wonder how women used to do this on their own, long ago. Oh yes. A lot of them died. I remember now. The babies, too.

Suddenly I am grateful for any sort of minor punishment that can be dished out. I happily give blood for the five hundredth time.

~

I'm arranging for my time off.

When I talked to my boss about it, I said twenty-four weeks. It sounded less like six months that way. I also told him I wanted to have a goodly time off before I came back to work, so that I could more fully be there, mentally, for the needs of the company. This is what is known as politics, baby.

I said that additionally, since I was planning to nurse, it would be best if you were off the breast before I came back to work.

My boss just looked at me dreamily and said, "That won't be for sixty years, at least."

Coworkers and strangers in coffee shops and everyone in elevators keep asking me when I'm due. I get asked about forty or fifty times a day. It's exhausting. It makes me think about labor and delivery, which is much like thinking about having a good long stroll over hot coals. I need someone to run PR.

I'm going to buy a chunky fake-gold medallion that says SEPTEMBER 14TH and wear it every day until delivery.

Thirty weeks.

I wait for the full realization of you to sweep over me in one astonishing wave, but it hasn't. Perhaps when my water breaks and I am officially in labor. I don't know if that will be enough, if pain or immediacy will provide the duct to you. You are so big, I can't know about you until you're here. My mind can't grasp it.

Today I was at Whole Foods and the bag girl said to the checkout clerk, "Is Pablo here?"

And the checkout woman said, "I don't know."

"He's here," I whispered, very low.

The checkout woman picked up a small handheld receiver and said into it, "PABLO TO THE FRONT END."

I wonder, was that what it was like in soul heaven when your time came to materialize?

"PABLO TO THE FRONT END."

You're five pounds now, the size of a chicken; I think of this whenever I buy chicken. It seems big enough to know about misogyny. There are some people who beat women up. Or tell them what to do, or act superior on an intellectual level, or any number of insulting unpleasantries aimed toward the female gender. You simply can't put a ceiling on how far these people are willing to go in order to prop themselves up, using any poor woman who happens to be in their immediate vicinity. Some of these people are women themselves. But most of them are men.

Of course, any man who feels he has to do these things is less of a man. Less of a human being. So let that be your measuring rod. The men who know how to respect women are the good men, the strong men. The other men have some deep psychological damage that renders them emotional-cripple monsters.

Ted Bundy is a good example. He was a serial killer in the 1970s, and he killed at least thirty women that we know about. At the end of his life in prison in Florida, he was bargaining to buy himself some more time by confessing to more crimes, but he ran out of days left on death row. They killed him by attaching a metal cap to his head and running electricity through him until he was cooked through.

When he saw a woman, a voice in his head used to say that she probably thought she was too good for him. That voice would persuade him to stalk her down whatever alley or street she was headed.

What Ted Bundy said about serial killing was "Gentlemen, there is no explaining it."

I think sexism is much the same, and homophobia and all the rest of it. You can explain some of it, but in the end it's a plain mystery, a disease that takes root and feeds off itself, ruining everything for its own sake. A rot.

Gentlemen, there is no explaining it.

Even then, he addressed only the men.

They say that Ted Bundy was very charming in his own way. While on death row, Ted got a woman to marry him, and they had a baby. Everyone was hugely relieved when it turned out to be a girl.

To his new wife, Ted seemed normal. Ted could make himself into whomever he needed to be. That's the one advantage of being insane; you can change a lot, until you have to wear the electrical hat.

On his last night, no one, not even his wife or mother, came to be with him. He died alone. I personally hope that every woman he had ever killed was waiting there on the other side with hot tongs, but maybe that makes me a little bit of a monster, too.

You make your own choice, to be a monster or a man. But know that women are your partners in humanity, and that next time you might just be one. Look out.

Eight months.

My inner compass seems to have suffered some sort of blow. I have become increasingly clumsy, even dangerous, in light of the life inside of me. A drunk is what comes to mind. Walking into walls, badly negotiating sharp-edged tables; even tall, blunt furniture seems to leap out at me from the sides of rooms, bashing itself against my shoulder as I try to pass. In addition, breathing seems to have become an advanced activity.

I call Diana, who is eight and a half months, and I ask her, "Do you have the *I can't breathe* thing?"

"No," she says, "I have the *I can't move* thing."

Not being able to breathe severely hinders gentility. Now, when total strangers ask me when I'm due, I have the irresistible urge to say, None of your Goddamn business, total stranger.

This just demonstrates my overall lack of evolution and how far I need to go before I can call myself spiritually cooked, baby. Before I can get on that big bus for nirvana.

We went and did the hospital tour last night. The first place they took us to was the lactation center, in fact a small, highly profitable retail shop for lace nursing bras, hardcover baby books, and $48.95 nightgowns with flaps that open at the breast. Far from making me feel disdain, this excited me. I will be able to send your father over there to buy us things. We'll be shopping as we go, baby. Then there's the regular gift shop, which has all sorts of other flamboyantly unnecessary items he may purchase.

Getting gifts is probably one of the best reasons to incarnate in the first place, and Mama is going to introduce you to it within your first hour, hour and a half, of life. As for myself, I'm trying to steer your father toward jewelry. Considering the pain and suffering, I don't think this is overkill.

Then they took us to the birthing suite, which I call the electronic bullshit room because it's full of all sorts of electronic bullshit we can't fathom but are just glad to have on principle.

The private and the double rooms have a Jacuzzi and a television and a phone by the bed, so I can't see anything to fear at all.
They sort of look like suites at the Four Seasons if you try a little.
Same peach-colored walls and bad art. I can't tell you how comforting that is for me.

The best part of the tour was swinging by the maternity ward,
where the fresh babies were coming out to be weighed. They looked
so astounding with their pointy heads and pink bodies; the charm
of the newborn is very, very strong. They looked like tiny fat naked
stockbrokers with attitudes, and somehow managed to be even cuter
than puppies. Your father looked through the glass for a minute
and said, "Those aren't the real babies. Those are the cute babies
that they put in the window for the tour. Those are the bait-and-
switch babies."

You will be one of them soon. You will emerge to great fan-
fare, and perhaps applause.

There's a certain kind of anarchy that's happening now. Your father goes to L.A. on business, and the first thing I do is go to the
supermarket and buy a Pepperidge Farm three-layer coconut cake.
It has this white frosting with coconut that's made with lard and
is brilliant. So I have a piece of that first thing in the door after
work, and then another slice after dinner, which usually involves
ground meat or a frozen fried-chicken Swanson monstrosity that
once again is entirely satisfying and delicious. The saltier and
the fattier and more loaded with white sugar, the better I seem to
like it. As I write this, I'm eating a grilled-cheese sandwich made
with Velveeta.

Diana called today. She's suddenly developed a late-third-trimester sinus infection that involves buckets of phlegm, which results in nausea.

"It was the worst cack I've ever had," she says. *Cack* is what she calls pregnancy vomit.

"It was just a waxy thread. Then I hurled about a quart of snot. Then it was the cacking because I cacked. The second wave."

It's three P.M. and she's lying on the bed on her left side, with the phone pressed to her right ear, the only position left to us beached-whale people, the only way we communicate. Her due date is very soon. Then Diana says, "I'll tell you right now, if I go into labor and I'm in an exhausted state? Epi."

Epidurals. We talk about them so much we have shortened them to *epi.* It's what they give women in labor when they begin to scream.

"Epi for sure," she says. "Knowing how hooked in to drugs I am, anyway. Because I am. I love them. I might as well come clean with that right now."

Your aunt Diana is the last honest woman alive. It's hard to find them, because they hide. But as I've said before, Diana is my best friend. A best friend is someone you trust, to whom you can say literally anything. I found mine at twelve. I hope you find yours even sooner.

Your father's mother called tonight and asked how I was, and your father simply said, "Big."

I feel inexorably defined by this bigness. Although it means you are growing and progressing, it also forces a distance between your father and me that is disconcerting. My bigness insulates me against him and the world, and no matter what, that extracts a toll.

There are certain blind places between a man and a woman, even your father and me, which I almost can't describe. Suffice it to say that sometimes being pregnant is fabulous and sometimes it is a dim and solitary time, and at the end this seems to intensify. It's not specific enough to say that, as a woman carrying you, I form an island of dual humanity, which by its very size and shape keeps others at bay. I myself am the island. Are islands lonely themselves? I believe so.

I don't think there are many men who would choose to be a woman. Your father, for one, has just today said that he wouldn't. Although I admire his candor, I was slightly taken aback by the vehemence with which he stated this. Perhaps seeing me this way has swayed him.

We could ask him another day.

A woman I know named Melodie Klein has just had her baby. She has the same doctor I have, Dr. Gray.

When the pain became intense, Melodie Klein asked for an epidural and was promptly administered one. She then skated on to a vaginal delivery without further incident. Within minutes, her baby girl tucked under her arm like a football, Melodie ordered fried rice on her cell phone and was checking her messages.

She was three centimeters dilated when she got the epidural.

Among my pregnant girlfriends and me, we now refer to this as The Legend of Melodie Klein. I covet her exact same experience, yet I have an uneasy hunch that if Melodie Klein has been spared pain, there will be more pain left over to be distributed among the rest of us.

What I want to do at the end of every day now is cry, from sheer physical exhaustion and also because I know that sleep will evade me and I won't be able to get comfortable no matter how many pillows I prop beneath my body. Also I know that I will not be held terribly close. It is impossible to hold an eight-months-pregnant woman close. Someday you might try and see for yourself. But to cry at the end of each day would be so tiresome for everyone that I don't. That's going to be your job when you arrive.

Just before he goes to sleep at night, your father says, "Good night, Pablo."

I am trying so hard to do this last bit right: for you, for your father, for everyone. It seems I don't want to jeopardize even a small portion of any one thing in order to do what comes naturally, which would be to lie down and give in, to lie down and possibly not get up again until you are born. *If* you are born.

Your father's mother, Simone, said that this is something I have in common with every woman, this crazy largesse, no matter how rich or poor. That we all go through this.

The question is: What do I have in common with the men?

Not you. I'm not talking about you, baby. You don't count as a strict man. What I have in common with you are cells. This body, this time. This grand-opening family. You will be my family in ways that no one else has been. You will be my blood family. Your father may be that for me also, but there are limits. In even the best of marriages, people are still separate. They cannot always hold you terribly close.

Now you know about the shadow of this side. If you grow up and are married and decide to make a baby, this all may come in handy. Remember to comfort your wife. She is the portal and portals, by definition, must narrow and darken. Must know they are only portals and not the thing itself. Must feel smaller than.

~

My belly button is about to go. It already looks different, more shallow, like the navel on an orange. It used to be deeper, more complex. Soon it will go, it will pop out, and then that's another passage, another sign. A going forward.

Your father says it's all grist for a great Broadway musical: "Bye-Bye Belly Button."

Twelve chorus girls in their final trimester.

FOUR STARS, SAYS BEN BRANTLEY. THE DANCING IS FANTASTIC.

~

Dr. Gray says you are in an oblique position now. You've moved out of breech and are on the diagonal to my stomach, your head just over my bladder. You heartbeat is low on my body, so this means you're hunkering down.

She also says you are of average size. We love that about you. How did I do on the ice test, she wants to know.

At the Lamaze class, they had me hold a block of ice for a full minute to simulate labor pain, saying "Hee-haw, hee-haw," and doing my breathing exercises. They make the husbands try it first. Your father made it through the whole minute. The vision of him shouting "Hee-haw," cross-eyed with pain, was singular. The first really great laugh I've had in weeks.

"So how long did you hold the ice?" Dr. Gray probes.

"Ten seconds," I admit.

"Then we have to think about an early epidural for you," she says.

"Early and often," I say.

I weigh one hundred and seventy-nine pounds. Interestingly enough, I've actually lost weight since my last visit. It's the fried chicken and white-flour-cake diet.

Your father has assembled the stroller. Also, the SUV has been purchased. You will have leather seats on which to spew.

I care less and less about work. All I care about now, really, is food. Everything else is the time in between food.

Tonight I'm going to have frozen fish fillet and macaroni and cheese, by Stouffer's. Carrot cake for dessert, the cheap Oregon Farms frozen kind. Then maybe some ridged potato chips with French-onion dip. Then who knows. The big question is no longer, "To be or not to be." Now the big question is, "What will I eat next?"

Last night you were moving and kicking for about three hours after dinner. Maybe it was the Tabasco sauce your father and I put on our fried chicken at Bubba's Diner. In any case, it was verging on the extremely unpleasant. You are either very energetic or are experiencing some sort of convulsions that I don't know about.

You put your left foot in, you put your left foot out. You do the hokey-pokey and you jam me in the ribs.

That's what it's all about.

We, the pregnant women who wait, comfort ourselves with labor bromides. My college friend Lia, who is nine months pregnant, calls me and says, "You know what I keep telling myself about labor? It's only a day . . . I can get through anything in one day. And! There are breaks in between the contractions."

She is selling me something I don't want to buy, but I have to, an iron lung.

"Oh yes, breaks," I say with deep sarcasm. "A few seconds to think about the coming pain." Then I tell her, "What I use to get me through this dread is a two-prong approach. Denial and medication. When the denial goes, send in the medication."

There is enormous pressure in California to have a baby without epidurals. Lia and I take umbrage at this on a political level. Also on the level of terror and cowardice.

Lia says, "If a man breaks his leg skiing, he doesn't go in to the emergency-room doctor and say, 'You know what? Let's do it the natural way. Let's set the leg without anesthesia.'"

For breakfast today I'm having strawberry shortcake from Max's Diner, which I got to go last night after your father and I ate dinner there (brisket sandwiches). It's a slab the size of a brick and has three layers of not just cake, strawberries, and whipped cream but custard as well.

I'm definitely taking an end-game approach to this thing. I have a very real sense that I may not survive childbirth anyway, so I'm getting my rewards now. Fuck it.

I've gained forty pounds. My doctor says this is good.

You sometimes give me knifing pains in my ribs when I attempt to sit up. I take it this means you are prospering.

I can't breathe when I lie on my back. It also requires a massive effort to turn over at night. If you turn a giant sea turtle on its back, it will die that way. It is unable to right itself.

I am in the giant-sea-turtle stage of the pregnancy. Except I don't get to die. In fact, if someone turns me over, I am able to commute to the office once again and create advertising.

We saw the rabbi today for my conversion process. She had a Magic 8-Ball on her desk.

We told her that the main reason we were doing this was because we wanted you to be something instead of nothing. She seemed to understand the wisdom of this and didn't press us for further explanation. The term *spiritual grounding* was wielded. You have to remember that this is the Marin Jewish Community Center, which means a lot of wavy-gravy terms. You'll see.

So you are going to be Jewish, baby. Eight days after you are born, there will be a *Bris.* Since we're not going to have you circumcised, you will have what your father calls a *Bris Lite,* without the traditional knife-the-penis section of the festivities. You will also have a naming ceremony in the synagogue. So will I when my training is complete, sometime around next summer.

Your father's Jewish name is Moishe. I never knew that until today when he told the rabbi. I hope mine is something pretty, like Rebekah, but it will probably more like Schmeckel.

I hope that Judaism appeals to you, but if not, feel free when you're ten or twelve years old to switch over to Buddhism or the Baha'i faith or agnostic. Naturally, I hope you don't go fundamentalist Christian or start hating Jews or boycotting Disney, but that's a possibility we're willing to live with. We don't want to tell you what to believe, we just want you to be something until you're something else. A primer coat.

I thought you were going to be among the first Jewish Pablos, but that was just my ignorance. Turns out there are a lot of Jewish Pablos worldwide, and in fact there was one in a recent film entitled *The Tango Lesson,* an actor named Pablo Verón who played a very handsome dancer who taught a thin white woman the tango. Pablo Verón was graceful and handsome and wicked: if you ask me, a very good argument for the Jewish Pablo.

When we were first trying to name you, I said, "What about Pablo?"

"Pablo," your father said, repeating it out loud. A bell went off; I was aware of a warmth in my stomach. That's how it happened.

I brought up some other names that I thought were nice, and your father raised his eyebrows and said, "What do you *mean?*" as though I were suggesting we flap our arms and fly to Narnia.

"I thought we had decided on Pablo," he said.

And that was that. We knew you were a Pablo and that was what you wanted to be, had always been meant to be. We saw how your life had its own shadowy yet distinct form, beginning with the right name, which had just now come to us from the future. As though time could be remembered forward.

Your godbrother has arrived into the world. Diana had her son, Dañiel Paz. He was born on his due date, the height of punctuality.

A new life. I cried, thinking about it, as your father and I were driving home from the lamp store. I turned my face to the window and hid my tears from him because I don't think he would understand.

You will cry, too, when you are born, but not for the same reasons that I will.

"It's all worth it," says Diana. "Everything."

Meanwhile, my baby shower was held on the hottest day of the year. A hundred and five degrees. About twelve women. Lia was the costar, she arrived looking elegant and not perspiring, even though she was mere moments from her due date.

You received many useful items, including a lambskin blanket, an ear thermometer, a fully coordinated outfit from Baby Gap, a grooming set, and a variety of other ridiculously small clothes. Your grandma gave you a brown teddy bear and $200, which we used for your stroller. It's important for a guy to have wheels.

You're in full launch position now. Head down into the pelvis. You haven't dropped yet, though. When you drop, it is rumored that I will be able to breathe again.

The doctor says you are above average size now. You gain an ounce every week until the birth.

Last night my feet were twitching and the mad ponies were after me. I moaned incessantly and drove your father from the room. Took a whole Xanax. It's every man for himself.

~

Today an account guy came into my office about a copy change, and I immediately said, "I'm not changing anything."

Don't fuck with me, I added into the silence. Another account guy in training looked on.

I should not still be working, obviously.

~

Lia had her baby on her exact due date. Vaginal delivery, no anesthesia. I just don't know if I am going to be able to be friends with her anymore.

I went to visit her, and she was looking gorgeous and half her old size, sitting up and eating Chinese food from the carton. Her son, Adam, was swaddled and tucked next to her in the bed as though he had always been there. He seemed to be humming to himself.

On the table next to her was the discarded hospital food and some magazines. Her husband, James, looked up from his seat, where he was happily slumped in a manner of a man who has run a race and won. He said, "Lia was magnificent."

I am so happy for her and so very depressed for myself. I want to be her. I want it to be over.

"I am so jealous," I say to Lia, all 182 pounds of me perched on the edge of the small hospital chair like Humpty Dumpty on the wall, knowing there is going to be a great fall. No way do I have Lia's strength. Lia is magnificent; I am just ordinary, or slightly below ordinary.

All the king's horses are going to have to haul ass, is what I think.

I am off work now, a week before your due date. I can feel you swinging your arms in the wings, waiting to come onstage. A sense of urgency has overtaken me. Restlessness streaks through my veins, it marbles my blood, my breath. Too pregnant to actually do anything, I have to wait. We both do.

After six hours of slight cramps, we drive to the hospital. The weather is good. It's a Friday. We stop at Lil's and have a ceremonial hamburger. I just eat the pickles and drink water.

We check in to the hospital, are placed in our birthing suite. Still the peach walls, the bad art. It's all good.

Ten hours of mild discomfort later, I am dilated to only three centimeters. They start me on Pitocin to induce stronger contractions. Dr. Gray visits, breezing in with an air of celebrity. She examines me, thinks it will be at least eight more hours until you are born. She breaks my water with what appears to be a plastic knitting needle. Warm amniotic fluid and blood oozes out of me, which feels good and scary all at once. Good-bye, water you lived in. Now you must be born. There is no going back.

The discomfort turns to actual pain about five minutes after the doctor breaks my water and leaves the room. It is not gradual.

Time passes. The pain is not just pain, it's a place. I am past the line of what is even remotely comfortable, and I am in the place of pain. A cruel and senseless purgatory from which no one, I feel certain, can emerge alive. I can't believe anyone would do this *twice*.

Around me in the hospital ward I hear women in various states of labor, moaning and cursing. Sudden screams echo down the hallway. This is madness, this is hell. This is not Pain with a Purpose. Lamaze class is crap.

In between contractions, I grip the bar on my hospital bed and clutch your father's hand, whining like a dog who has been hit by a car. Your father says labor is bad, but he knows something worse. "What?" I say. He smiles gently and says, "Death by *Titanic* theme song."

I have just received an epidural, after seven and a half hours of regular and even labor. And nothing has happened, the promised relief has not come.

The contractions are coming every thirty seconds and I am still feeling them, the pain is actually accelerating, which horrifies me. I want to scream, not only from pain but from the thought of the pain to come, which is going to be worse, unbearable. Your father walks two steps away from the bedside and I say, "Come back." I need him to survive this. He is my link to the outside world, the place outside the pain. And the anesthesiologist is saying with obvious impatience, "It's supposed to hurt. You're supposed to feel some pain."

I am very depressed now. The epidural didn't work. How can it not work? And why doesn't the anesthesiologist believe me?

"He thinks I'm lying," I tell the nurse, Susan. She is angry with him and steps outside the room to discuss the problem with him, telling him that something has not worked correctly. Telling him, I presume, that he has *missed*. I hear him arguing that he did not miss, that I am just experiencing oversensitivity.

"*Bull*shit," Susan says, her voice harsh. "It is not supposed to hurt like that."

Finally he walks back in and tells me in a loud, clear voice, as though I have gone senile, that he will go and do another epidural on a woman down the hall. And then he will come back, and if I still need another one, he'll do it again. He is making deals. I have no choice. I agree, I accept the deal. *I'll take Pain and Suffering for five hundred.*

More agony and *then* more drugs: it's his schedule. I am merely a stop on his schedule. There are other women contorted in pain for him to get to, other women he must straighten. The anesthesiologist is our savior. Cruel or just, there is no other.

I don't believe that he is coming back. I would like to harm him, to whack his stomach with a bat so he understands, so he wipes that scorn off his face, his relaxed, pain-free, bland face, but I cannot because he is my only hope of escaping the pain. I say to him, "Promise you'll come back." "I will," he says. It's like a bad love story. He leaves.

There is more pain, one contiguous contraction that ebbs and flows with the fierce precision of time itself. I watch the clock, misery and disbelief washing over me in constant waves. No one prepared me for this. I should have been practicing by ripping fingernails out every night for a week. Passing a cheese grater repeatedly over my tongue.

Two hours later the anesthesiologist has returned, cheerful and sheepish. I am writhing.

"I guess it didn't take," he admits, laying out his instruments. "Let's try this again."

I have the second epidural and it works right away, it goes into the right place and the pain instantly recedes and is gone, like a fresh blood stain in ice water. And everyone is relieved, your father is relieved and I am relieved; except when I try to move at all, I can't. It seems the anesthesiologist has given me more than an average dose of medication in the fear that I may be resistant to the drugs. He didn't really miss on the first one, in other words; I am simply insensitive.

As a result of the dosage, I can't move at all, and this panics me. I have settled in an awkward position and my back twists, but I can't readjust my position. I am deeply uncomfortable and no one cares, they're wrapping me in a blanket and saying, "Sleep now. Rest." I am far from feeling restful, I am the opposite of sleepy, my mind is screaming with anxiety and I do not know why.

Then the fetal monitor, which gauges your heartbeat, begins to slow. There was no prelude, it just suddenly dipped and then we are all staring at the monitor. Beep . . . beep . . . beep. In three or four seconds it goes from 150 beats per minute to 125, and then to 95. I hear this happen, and through my initial shock, it registers what this sound means, my mind takes it in and freezes solid.

"Turn her over!" the nurse shouts, and they are lifting me and turning me over. I can't help, because I am paralyzed. I have lost all power. I feel like an observer, except I am terrified in a way that an observer cannot be.

Eighty-five beats per minute.

They are pushing the buttons on the headboard, paging for help. "Do you need a doctor?" a voice shouts from the intercom. "*Yes,* we need a doctor," the nurse says. She is not talking, she is shouting.

"I'm scared," I say to your father. I grip his hand. "I'm scared." My brain has seized, I can only repeat simple declarative sentences. His face is the color of rain.

"Help," I say, to no one. Nurses fly about the room like witches, unplugging me from the IV and the Pitocin drip.

In the eye of this, there seems to be a cruel well of time. I think of your last sonogram photo, your plump-lipped, Hitchcock profile. I think of your crib with its clean clothes pressed into white drawers. I have a sudden yet sure conviction that you are me; I am dying. I hear you/me dying.

Beep . . . beep . . .

Eighty beats per minute.

"Get any doctor in here *now*," your father shouts suddenly. He is being forceful with strangers. He is never forceful with strangers. He is gracious and well mannered with strangers. But now he is someone else. Shock has knocked me out to a vicinity somewhere above my prone body.

A man with white hair runs into the room, a doctor who is a stranger. In my entire life I have never been so glad to see anyone. He looks not at us but straight at the fetal monitor and says, "How long has this been going on?" He does not look at me. I am the husk. You are what matters. I accept this. I will give my life for you if necessary. My life for yours. Just let your heart speed up again.

I am praying, but what I am also thinking is: You cannot do this, God. You grisly motherfucker, you cannot *do this*.

"Ten minutes," the nurse, Susan, says. "It's been ten minutes." It has not been ten minutes, it has not been more than three minutes. But she is not taking any chances, she wants him to hurry. She is not making the deal. Do something, her body quietly implores.

Suddenly Dr. Gray runs in. "What's happening?" she asks. It is the first time I have ever seen her face uncertain.

"The baby's crashing," Susan says.

Not happening, I think.

"We're going to take you in to O.R. and then we'll reassess," the silver-haired doctor says, leaning down into my face. Oh, this soft language.

"Oxygen," I say, nodding yes to reassessment as I realize I can't breathe.

They unplug me from the fetal monitor and they run me down the hall, an oxygen mask on my tearless face. They are running, and I think, This is a scene from a hospital drama, any moment George Clooney is going to sidle up to me and squeeze my hand and whisper, "Don't worry," and something flirty and kind, but he doesn't. George Clooney isn't coming because this is not a hospital drama, it is actually happening.

Can't be happening, intones my brain. Can't.

Oh yes, the lights on top of the ceilings say, and the wheels and edges of my horror sled bash the wall as the doctors rush the gurney around corners. Oh yes it can.

I don't see your father anywhere. He is running behind us, they are pushing him out of the way. And I don't realize this until we get into the O.R. and I say, "Where's my husband?" And they say, "He's out in the hallway, he can't come in now." "Is my husband all right?" I ask. Instead of becoming more people, we are becoming fewer.

"Outside," they say, as they rush to reattach the fetal monitors. I hear your heartbeat, and it is so slow.

I beg them to cut you out, to save you. "Get him out of me," I say. "Get him *out*."

Dr. Gray comes into view above the tubes and monitors. "We're going to do a C-section because the baby is running out of gas."

"Hurry," I say, agonized that she is taking this moment to explain. "Hurry."

As I am hastily prepared for surgery, the anesthesiologist chides Susan, the nurse, for not putting the vital-sign monitors on my chest. "I'm not here to do your job," she barks. She has had it with him. Everyone is losing control. Chaos has opened. I can hear your heartbeat again. It sounds slower.

I am praying for the general anesthesia now, praying to go under. Because I can't listen to this any longer, can't bear it. Your heart is on its way to stopping. And the mask is coming down and I will leave. I absolutely must leave.

"Breathe deeply," a voice says, a hand on my face. "deeply."

I breathe deeply. I inhale oblivion, meeting a last hope that surprises me in the darkness, like dawn.

And gone.

After surgery I emerge to pain across my stomach, a sharp line that has me in its vise.

"We've got a thrasher," I hear them say. I say, "It hurts, it hurts." I am throwing my limbs about, trying to sit up. I need to sit up. I don't know why.

"Calm down, you've got to lie down," they say. Gloved hands push me down. "Rest."

"It hurts, it hurts," I exclaim. Need to sit up. Get away. I am an animal. I have no thoughts. I remember nothing except that I have this line of pain and it is not right. I will harm anyone who comes near me.

I go out again.

I wake up and your father is standing next to me. His face is slick with tears and he is saying something. Something, I realize, about you.

Sobs are coming out of me. "Mark," I say. "Mark." His name washes over me like water. I try to sit up again. He holds my shoulders gently as he speaks.

"You have a beautiful baby boy."

"Thank God," I say. I see now why this is written into every script. They are the two words that must be said, that are automatic.

And then blackness again.

~

I awake in ICU. Your father has gone to see you in the nursery.

The incision is a streak of fire across my belly. I cry out for a nurse, who summons the Man. The one with the drugs.

He quietly explains, "If we give you morphine, you could stop breathing."

"Please give me something." I realize distantly that I am begging. "Well . . ." he says. More deals.

The anesthesiologist converses briefly with the head nurse, and then he smiles and says he can give me some morphine after all, a small amount. He attaches a clear vial of morphine into my IV and it begins to enter my bloodstream, and I can immediately think again. I love the morphine and the person who invented it. I love everyone, including . . . no, *especially* the anesthesiologist. The terror of the experience is draining out of me, the realization of you slowly filling me. I have not seen you. Still I rise into the air, a balloon of happiness.

The head nurse comes up to me, smiles, and rubs her hand in a small circle on my sternum. It is ineffably comforting.

Then she says, "Normally we would bring the baby in to see you, but . . ."

Across the thin blue ICU curtain, I hear moans and the sounds of someone coming out of anesthesia.

I look at the nurse. Her eyes are sad. They come from a merciless place where truth is black and yet must be spoken.

"The woman next to you," she whispers, "has just lost her baby."

Lost, I think, stupidly, fresh grief washing over me. No, not lost, I think. One loses a button, one does not lose a baby. Surely they are taken from us.

"May we bring your son into your room later?" she wants to know.

"Of course," I say to the nurse. "Of course I can wait." Waiting is nothing. You're out there, alive. I feel a wild relief, and then shame. Terrible shame, to have drawn the white stone.

Rustling sounds from just beyond the operating-room curtain that separates us. I cannot imagine her pain. I cannot imagine how she will live. In a morphine fog, I flinch against the dark hook of something implacable in the room with us, something that has come not out of evil but some terrible mercy. "The baby," the nurse whispers, "had multiple coronary anomalies." A heart not made for this world.

They say that as women, we are designed by nature to forget the details of childbirth. Nothing could be more false. She will not forget this. I will not forget this. A woman whom I will never meet has shared your birth, has marked it with her blood, the blood of childbirth. Blood that, I see now, was always there but hidden. Hidden.

You are born, I tell myself. Found. Tears coat the sides of my face.

I observe how slender the line is between life and death. This thin blue curtain that travels on small metal rings.

You entered the world at 3:01 P.M. Your umbilical cord was wrapped twice around your neck, prolapsed and wedged against the placenta. After resuscitation, your Apgar scores were four and nine. You weighed seven pounds and seven ounces. In another time or place, you would not have survived birth, would have strangled on your own cord.

Two hours and five minutes after you are born, they bring you to my room. Room 250. I hold out my hands. You look at me, an olive bundle with brown wispy hair that looks as though it was recently styled. You have the slanted eyes of my father, and your father's full lips and broad neck. There is a dimple in your chin, which we all find highly remarkable, as though you have been born with shoes.

"Where did you come from?" I ask. I can't believe you.

"Hello," I say. "Baby."

But you are not a baby, you are a full-size being in a small body. Already I know that. Those are not the eyes of a baby. I have not made you. I am just the house. You are home. We are all finally, I know as you clutch my forefinger in your perfect hand, home.

"What did you do while I was unconscious?" I ask Mark later.

"They told me to put on scrubs, which got caught on my shoes because I didn't take my sandals off, and finally I got the scrubs on. But then they said I couldn't come into the operating room, it was happening too fast and I had to wait outside. I stepped into the hall, and a minute later they told me they needed the birthing suite for another woman, and so I had to go clean out the room right away."

Hearing this at first, I would like to upbraid someone. But then I understand that maybe doing something is better than doing nothing. And there were women in labor waiting for that room.

"I was in there praying and saying, 'Whatever you want of me, I'll do it if you will just make my wife and baby all right.' And I was blaming myself for everything I had ever done wrong, thinking that's what had caused this terrible thing to occur. Meanwhile, I was stuffing your clothing into your suitcase and trying to round up everything.

"I had just finished when a nurse ran in and said, 'Mother and baby are doing fine.'"

"What did you do?" I ask.

"I said, 'Thank you,'" he says. "The nurse said, 'You're welcome.' Then I burst into tears."

I was not here to usher you into the world. But your father was. Your grandmother took a picture of you in the nursery, your father holding you as you scream, clearly furious. On his face is an expression of deep tenderness; he is looking directly into the camera and at the same time seems beyond it. He looks younger.

That night, after many other pictures have been taken, the ecstatic grandparents have come and gone, insisting on videoing you while you yawn. Your father has gone to sleep on a cot next to my bed. A woman in white comes quietly into the room.

"What's his name?" the nurse asks as she checks my catheter.

"Pablo," I say. Keeping your other, Jewish name secret. In case anyone or thing comes looking for you; tries to take you back, to call you lost. But you I will tell.

Your Jewish name is Chaim.

This means *life*.

The Seed Market

Can you find another market like this?

Where,
with your one rose
you can buy hundreds of rose gardens?

Where,
for one seed
you get a whole wilderness?

For one weak breath,
the divine wind?

You've been fearful
of being absorbed in the ground,
or drawn up by the air.

Now, your waterbead lets go
and drops into the ocean,
where it came from.

It no longer has the form it had,
but it's still water.
The essence is the same.

This giving up is not a repenting.
It's a deep honoring of yourself.

When the ocean comes to you as a lover,
marry, at once, quickly,
for God's sake!

Don't postpone it!
Existence has no better gift.

No amount of searching
will find this.

A perfect falcon, for no reason,
has landed on your shoulder,
and become yours.

—Rumi

Acknowledgments

Once again, people in New York have made themselves indispensable. My agent, Kim Witherspoon, continues to be as close to Athena as humanly possible. My sublime and indefatigable editor, Elisabeth Schmitz, kept me from harm in ways too numerous to list, as did Beth Thomas. Many thanks to Morgan Entrekin at Grove/Atlantic, home of subversive writers everywhere. Andrew Robinson, Sean Mullens, Augusten Burroughs, Sabrina Bourg, Sally Willcox, Molly Boren, Lauren Wein, Bunny and Ron Mathews, Jill Murray, Lynda Pearson, Ken Woodard, Lisa Summers, and Arthur "Ain't Too Proud to Scan" Vibert, and my jackpot sibling, Dee Alexich, provided inspiration. I owe Thom Gunn for the beginning time; Annie was there when I was falling. To the Irish day nurse at the hospital whose name I have forgotten but whose grace I have not. And mostly to my son, Pablo, for choosing me to come through.